CRY OF THE GOSHAWK

To Christopher,
Roy W. Bush
4/04/07

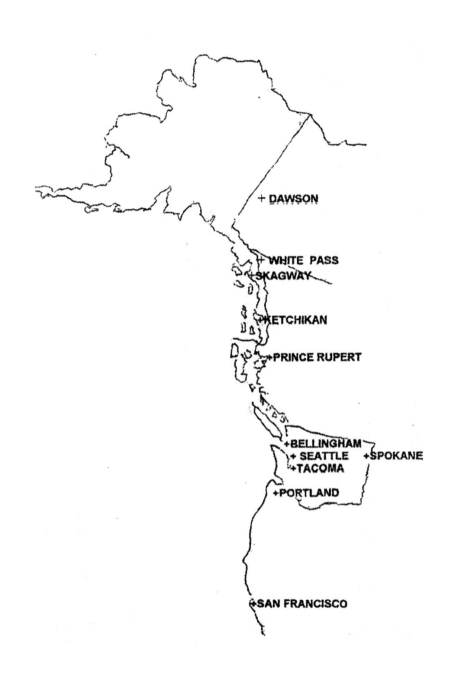

CRY
OF THE
GOSHAWK

(gos'hawk)

A Casey Jones Adventure

Roy Bush

ELDERBERRY PRESS, INC.

Copyright © 2006 Roy Bush

All rights reserved. No part of this publication, except brief excerpts for purpose of review, may be reproduced, stored in a retrieval system, or transmitted in any form or by any means, electronic, mechanical, photocopying, recording, or otherwise, without the prior written permission of the publisher.
This is a work of fiction. Any resemblance of the characters to persons living or dead is purely coincidental.
Illustrated by Raven OKccfc
Elderberry Press, Inc.
1393 Old Homestead Drive, Second Floor
Oakland, Oregon 97462–9506.
E MAIL: editor@elderberrypress.com
TEL/FAX: 541. 459. 6043
www. elderberrypress.com

Available from your favorite bookstore, amazon.com, or from our 24- hour order line: 1. 800. 431. 1579

Library of Congress Control Number: 2006927329
Publisher's Catalog—in—Publication Data
Cry of the Goshawk / Roy Bush
ISBN 10: 1932762639
ISBN 13: 978-1-932762-63-1
1. Young Adult—Fiction.
2. Adventure—Fiction.
3. Dogs—Fiction.
4. Coming of Age—Fiction.
5. Boy's Adventures—Fiction.
I. Title

This book was written, printed and bound in the United States of America.

My thanks to Ann Saling, for her encouragement through the
Pacific Northwest Writers Association,
and to Inga Wiehl for her patient editorial assistance.

To Dorothy, my wife and inspiration.

one

MY TRAIN WRECK

CASEY

I'll always remember the summer of 1920. My dad died, and I still re-live the dark days when my mom and I struggled to get our lives back on track. I couldn't help to support us. . . no job anywhere for a boy of sixteen that would pay enough. So now I'm on my way out west to live with my aunt. In a few hours, this train will roll into Seattle.

At first, thoughts of Mom and my friends back in Brooklyn crowded out everything else. But when I changed trains in Chicago, I sat next to this nice-looking guy. I watched him put his tan, tattered suitcase under the seat. I thought talking to him might get my mind off myself.

"Hi, I'm Casey Jones," I began.

"Hello, I'm Benny from the Bronx." He smiled and added, "Any relation to the famous railroader?"

Because I have the same name as an Illinois Central engineer who died trying to avoid a train wreck, I always get this question.

"No, Jones is a common name."

Benny continued eagerly, "I'm goin' to Seattle . . . gotta job on a fishing boat . . . might even make it up to Alaska."

Benny, who settled in with a sigh, seemed to be in his early twenties; with his slim, lanky frame, he looked hungry.

"Fishing in Alaska . . . that sounds exciting."

As the train clacked over the tracks, I sat back on the green, plush seat and wondered about sailing out to sea, fishing for a living. I longed for adventure; something that would give my life a lift, like standing on the deck, pole in hand, as a huge fish took the bait. My arm muscles tensed, as, in my mind, the line gave a mighty jerk. Braced on the ship's rail, I struggled to reel in a huge, silvery salmon, then flipped it, flopping and flashing, into a waiting tub. The captain gave me a smiling thumbs-up just before the train gave a jerk, and I came back to reality. I wanted to stay aboard the boat . . . bait the hook, cast it in the frothy foam and challenge the sea for another catch. But my vivid vision evaporated. Instead of fresh, ocean air, I breathed cigar smoke mixed with fumes from our coal-burning engine.

Well, so much for my dandy day-dream.

I turned to Benny. "I'd rather be catching fish aboard a boat than slicing them up in a Seattle sea-food shop."

Benny's dark eyes went wide with surprise. "You're going to work in a fish market?"

"Yes, from what my aunt wrote, it looks that way." I slipped Aunt Minnie's letter from my shirt pocket. "Listen to this, Benny: 'Casey can use our spare bedroom . . . and maybe he'll find it interesting to help out in his Uncle Carl's sea-food business this summer.'"

Benny's whole face wrinkled into a big smile. "Well, looks like I'll be catchin' 'em and you'll be cleanin' 'em and sellin' 'em."

I had to laugh. "And the moms will be fryin' 'em and everybody'll be eatin' 'em."

Benny welcomed a little humor, guffawed and poked me on shoulder. "Haw! Between the two of us, we'll have folks eatin' so much fish, it'll be a comin' outa their ears!"

Laughing helped lighten up my dark mood. But still, I couldn't forget the strong smell of the Fulton Fish Market in lower Manhattan.

I hoped for the best. On the job I'd probably get used to smelling fish, and maybe I'll get to go to high school too.

As we talked, the home-sick lump in my stomach melted away. Benny'd left New York to start a new life, too. Maybe we could get together in Seattle before he sailed for Alaska.

I told myself, "You're dreaming again! Seattle's a big place. When we get off the train we'll go our separate ways and I'll never see Benny again."

I looked out at the passing countryside from my window seat. In a way, my whole life seemed to be rushing by.

What would my life with Aunt Minnie and Uncle Carl be like? Would school be a part of it? Already I missed my classes back in Brooklyn . . . especially the interesting new electronic stuff produced by the inventor, Edison, and a scientist named Tesla.

I thought of old Mr. Lambrusco who lived in our apartment house. What a wonderful neighbor. He taught me to juggle, to play his mandolin, and loaned me fascinating geography and history books that showed how the explorers opened up the new world. Well, if I can't go to school, at least maybe there'll be a library nearby.

These last two days Benny and I had rolled through the mostly flat land of Montana, then crossed the Rocky Mountains. Now, as we raced though eastern Washington I noticed a big change in the landscape . . . and it wasn't what I expected.

Back in Brooklyn, the principal's parting comment was, "You'd better pack an umbrella, Casey, Seattle gets as much rain as London." Checking me out for a three-thousand-mile journey brought out the teacher in him. He added, "Wet, maritime climate there, you know." From that, I expected to see lush greenery about now. Instead, my eyes traveled out to a treeless countryside. Rain? Maritime climate? Not out there! Dry, desolate desert rolled by. Even the sparse sagebrush, which extended out to the distant hills, looked dead. I'll bet if a drop of rain hit that scrubby stuff, it would explode. London? Forget the umbrella! This country is more like the Sahara!

I refused to be depressed by the dreary desert. We didn't own an umbrella anyhow. A thought made me smile: "This part of the west is not exactly as bright and colorful as those patchwork quilts Mom made to cover our beds back in Brooklyn."

In New York City the sidewalks run up and down; one like another, but the buildings are different and the neighborhoods with their six-story apartment houses, little shops and parks, have a sameness about them. Then I thought of the view from the Staten Island ferry . . . the big bridges, Ellis Island and the Statue of Liberty, so different from this strange land out there.

An unpainted house came into view. Two black horses cantered about in a split-rail corral.

"Aha! I thought, "There is life out there." I liked horses, and drank in the sight of them. In New York, motor cars were replacing them, but the big city still had horse-drawn carts. A strange idea began to push its way into my mind like grass sprouting between the cracks of a sidewalk. For days now, this train had rolled on through cluttered cities, thick forests, and vast prairies . . . on and on . . . I began to think we'd overshot the west coast and somehow wound up in another land entirely. As the corral passed by, my imagination began to gallop. Maybe we've run off the face of the earth to another planet. Except for the little farm, it was more like Mars out there than planet earth.

I bumped my head against the thick window a couple of

times to get reality going again. Living out there would be like dying and finding yourself in the "hot place!" I couldn't think of a landscape more unpleasant. At least in the Sahara, one could find a green oasis and palm trees. I leaned back and closed my eyes, overcome by thoughts of sun-scorched sands. Minutes later a sudden squeal of brakes snapped me back to reality.

Our single set of tracks had become two as our train entered a huge rail yard with hundreds of boxcars. Several small switch engines puffed smoke and pushed lines of cars. The train slowed, yet buildings rushed by; some were built of brick. We were stopping at a large town. I thought, "Maybe the train station will have a news-stand and candy counter." My mouth watered at the thought of peanuts and chocolate as I eagerly pulled a nickel from my pocket.

When we lurched to a stop I jumped past Benny into the aisle, ahead of a woman and a little boy, ran to the vestibule between the cars, and clamored down behind the conductor to the brick platform.

On the platform the arrival of our passenger train had stirred things up. With the engine bell clanging, and pistons hissing steam, there was an air of excitement all about. Uniformed porters in red hats pulled their clattering green freight wagons, loaded with mail and baggage, to the freight cars ahead.

The air was pungent with smoke from our big locomotive that sat snorting a protest of pent-up power like a huge animal, eager to charge back onto the prairie. A thrill of excitement shot through me with a premonition that something big was about to happen.

The conductor checked his pocket watch. I knew I had only a few minutes, then the train would leave, with or without me. I sure didn't want to be stranded in this strange place. And what would Aunt Minnie think if I didn't arrive as expected?

I rubbed the buffalo on my nickel and squinted against the

sun at the large, open area inside the depot. I could see no sign of a magazine counter . . no candy bar here. Disappointed, I turned back and became caught up in all the activity around me until the trainman called out, "All aboard!"

But just then, a large middle-aged man bore down on me like a steam engine. I panicked at his fierce expression, spun around and scrambled back, but the stranger caught my arm in an iron grip. We had suddenly come together, even though, like the other Casey Jones, I'd tried to avoid a collision.

My nickel flew away, bouncing under the train. No matter. My roiling stomach wasn't wanting candy now; the big man had jerked me back with such force, I'd almost lost my lunch.

"Boy, is your name Casey?"

"Y-yes," I gulped, with a voice pitched two octaves higher than normal.

With his red face close to mine, he barked, "I'm your Uncle Harry and you're coming with me!"

The conductor, a few feet away, gave the signal for the train to move out. Uncle Harry barked again, this time at the startled trainman.

"Do you know where this boy was sitting?"

"Yes."

"I'm Harry Kinsman, his uncle. I have authority to take him off the train. His mother says he has just one bag. Go find it and throw it off!"

When the conductor heard the name Harry Kinsman, he snapped to attention like an army private. He leaped on board to fetch my bag, and I heard, "TOOT, TOOT," then the "CLANG" of a freight car door rumbling shut.

Uncle Harry wasn't taking any chances. Now that he had me, he wasn't about to let me get away. With an eye on the train, he tightened his grip.

How could I have imagined this wild train wreck of sorts?

Here on a railroad platform miles from home, I'd collided with an uncle I'd never met.

two

HIT BY HATE

UNCLE HARRY

The train began to leave the station. As it picked up speed, Uncle Harry released me. I stood there rubbing the circulation back in my arm, and thought of my bag of clothes and keepsakes that were fast escaping to Seattle. Oh, how I longed to be with them. I hadn't even said goodbye to Benny.

I'd tried to look on the bright side of things, and talking to Benny had helped. But now, my thoughts returned to last month. I'd tried to be strong and help Mom when my dad had died after an appendicitis operation. I'd thought, "It's just the two of us now in the big, uncaring city. I have to grow up fast." But during the long, dark nights I couldn't hold back the tears. I'd finally slip off to sleep whispering, "Why? Why did you do it, Dad?"

After the operation, he'd gone back to work shoveling coal at the foundry. It had been too soon. Too soon! Now, thousands of miles from home, I fought down sobs rising in my throat as I watched the train, Benny, and my bag move away, leaving me behind. What would my dad have said about all this? Dad, so handsome, with his wavy brown hair and thick mustache.

I used to love it when he would come home from work.

When I was younger I'd run to him and he'd swing me around. He'd laugh a greeting. "How's my Casey from Canarsie? You been good to your mother?" Now, in a strange western town, I wiped my eyes with my sleeve.

I had a flashback to when Dad's foreman at the steel foundry sat in our little parlor and told Mom the awful details of how Dad had died. "I knew something was wrong," he'd said, "when your husband, Dan, dropped his coal shovel and grabbed his side with both hands . . . trying to keep his guts in, he was." Mom's face became pale with grief. The foreman finally finished. "Sure sorry ma'am, Dan'd pulled his stitches loose – bled to death right there on the job. We just couldn't help him." On his way out, the foreman handed over a stained envelope. "We took up a collection for you and the boy."

Mom found a job as a clerk, but it didn't pay much. When Aunt Minnie and Uncle Carl offered to take me, I had to go.

Now, on the depot platform, I felt light-headed and my heart was pounding. As I raised my hand to the letter in my shirt pocket, I wondered if I'd ever get to meet Aunt Minnie or see Seattle.

The conductor appeared at the last second and smoothly slid my canvas suitcase from the moving train onto the platform. I bolted down the track to pick it up, happy to retrieve something familiar. I hugged my bag of belongings and turned back to . . . I knew not what.

I'd heard very little about my mother's brother, Harry. I looked him in the eye as he stood waiting for me. His thick crop of black hair and heavy mustache showed hints of gray. His dark suit and tie gave him a professional look. As he returned my gaze, his stern expression slowly relaxed into a smile. I walked up to him and smiled back.

Showing some kindness, he placed a gentle hand on my shoulder. "I sent your Aunt Minnie a telegram. She knows about this change of plans."

We headed for a Model T Ford with its top down, and he continued. "Your mother knows too." Uncle Harry's attempt to reassure me helped to calm my riled-up stomach. "That's my car there at the curb."

Were we going to drive to some dry farm, out in the "dead" country? The thought gave me chills on a hot day.

I climbed in, still clutching my bag, as Uncle Harry stepped around in front and cranked the Model T to a start. The car bounced as he hopped in and began to drive smoothly through what seemed to be the main part of town. I was pleased to see the streets were paved and curbed too. There were neat shops with offices over them. I caught the name of the newspaper as we drove by, The Arborville Grapevine. I thought, "So now I know the name of this place . . . Arborville."

Uncle Harry spoke up. "Right now, we're heading to my place, Casey. You'll meet your Aunt Louise." In a gentle tone of voice he added almost under his breath, "and your cousins too, if they're at home."

Cousins! I dimly remembered that my mom's brother, Harry, had three daughters, or was it four? My head began to swim again. Uncle Harry continued. "You will be living with us now. We have plenty of room and we're better able to provide a true home for you than your Aunt Minnie in Seattle."

I heaved a sigh. I'd been looking forward to living in Seattle. But now I wouldn't be cleaning fish. For all I knew, that fish market might be the nearest one of its kind to Arborville.

There were few cars around, and some horse-drawn wagons gave the town a true western flavor. The sign above one quaint shop read: J. J. Magnusson's Son—Harness Shop. I also noticed a larger building with two signs, one mounted vertically high on the corner and the other across the front. Both read: Hotel Bellmont. People on the street were dressed countrified; women and girls in blouses and long skirts; men and boys in overalls. Some of the men, however, probably shopkeepers or professional men, wore suits with vests and black string ties.

I'd just begun to relax and appreciate the ride with all the strange sights, when my attention was riveted on a young man standing on the sidewalk. As we passed, his menacing stare threw a scare into me. He stood with clenched fists and his eyes met mine in an unblinking glare of hate. When I glanced back over my shoulder, his whole face contorted into a fearful grimace. My heart began to pound again. When I closed my eyes, I could still see the round, menacing, face, under a tweed cap worn low to black eyebrows.

My mind raced for answers. Why had my uncle pulled me off the train? Had my mother and Aunt Minnie really agreed to my coming here to Arborville instead of going to Seattle? The biggest question I spoke out loud, "Who was that scowling young man, and why was he glaring at me?"

I wasn't sure that Uncle Harry heard me ask that question over the staccato sound of the motor, but he'd seen the young man too. He leaned over and said in a loud voice, "That was just Vernon. He's a ne'er-do-well. Take my advice, ignore him."

This time Uncle Harry didn't help my apprehensive mood much. Ignore him? Would I be able to do that? I truly hoped so.

Still light-headed, I wished that I'd eaten a candy bar to pep me up for whatever might come next. I'd had little to eat since the train had pulled out of Spokane, only a light lunch of a dry roll, the last piece of salami I'd brought along, and a cup of coffee I'd bought from the porter for 10 cents. I was relieved when we pulled up to the garage of a large, two-story brick home, with a sweeping front lawn and fine shade trees.

I wiped the sweat from my brow. Whew! Not the Sahara!

Uncle Harry switched off the motor and yelled, "Here we

are, Casey!" He jumped down, leaving me to scramble out with my bag. I pulled my cap off and followed as Uncle Harry strode around to the front door of his impressive home.

There, to greet us, stood a tall, beautiful woman with blond braids wound neatly on top of her head.

Uncle Harry began, "Casey, this is your Aunt Louise." Then he grabbed me to stand in front of him: "Louise, my dear, this fine young lad is my sister's son, Casey Jones."

She took my hand in both of hers. "Hello, Casey," she said warmly, "I'm so very pleased to meet you. Welcome to our home. We call it Overton Manor. We have a meal ready for you. I expect you must be famished after the long train ride."

Before I could respond, a cute girl ran right up to me and gave me a big hug. She seemed about my age, if not younger. She sparkled with cheerfulness. "Hello, Casey," she laughed. "I'm your cousin Colette."

three

AMBUSHED

AUNT LOUISE

Seated alone at the large dining room table, I met the maid, Sally, as she brought my meal, served on beautiful dishes. Middle-aged and medium-sized, she wore a blue and white striped apron and a kind expression.

As Sally put a plate of pot roast, small red potatoes and green beans in front me, I thought, "Hmm, the Kinsmans eat well." I poured a generous amount of rich brown gravy over everything. Sally, who doubled as the cook, nodded her approval.

"You'll be needing a glass of milk, I think."

"Yes, thank you."

Sally continued, "Apple pie for dessert?"

With a full mouth, I nodded emphatically.

Minutes later, I cleaned up the last bit of gravy with a bit of bread and wiped my mouth on a huge linen napkin.

Like magic, a large slice of apple pie came sailing over my left shoulder, served by Sally who'd been hovering nearby.

Fork flying, I tied into the pie.

"Can you think of anything else, young man?"

I hesitated.

"Now, now," Sally said encouragingly. "Your first meal here should lack nothing. What else? A few after-dinner mints, perhaps?"

Sally looked at me so kindly, I couldn't resist blurting out, "Some black coffee maybe?"

"Coffee?" Sally raised her blond eyebrows in surprise. "Well, now. We have a fresh pot on the stove. You shall have your coffee!"

Though I was large for my age, Sally must have thought me a bit young for coffee. I decided that my cousins probably didn't drink coffee.

I thought of Colette, who'd kind of bowled me over and then had left as quickly as she'd come. I was nervous about meeting others. What would they think of me?

When I'd finished my coffee, Sally led the way up a curved staircase and down a short hallway to a large room where my old suitcase had been placed on a rack by the double bed.

"Skidoo!" I said out loud. "What a terrific bedroom!" Impressed by a desk with a bookcase over it, I loved the pictures of blue-green ocean scenes on the walls.

The view from the window overlooked dozens of homes below, all surrounded by neat lawns and colorful flowers. Farther out, I expected to see more dry, desert country, but instead, several farms, many with grapevines, extended out to green hills.

"I've not landed in the hot place," I thought. "This is more like heaven!"

Below the open window, I heard Mrs. Kinsman call out, "Sally, have you seen Annabell?"

"Yes, ma'am. She's out in the garden."

As I began to unpack, I noticed my Brooklyn Dodgers shirt. Would I ever see another game at Ebbets field? With pitchers like Burleigh Grimes, who'd already won 20 games, and 300-hitters like Zack Wheat, they'd probably finish in first place. Sad to miss the rest of the season, I picked up another shirt to change into.

I found the upstairs bathroom and, after a refreshing shower and a change of clothes, I was eager to look around.

Overton Manor's grassy grounds sloped gently to the main gate in front. I wandered around back to a large vegetable garden.

I loved the earthy smell of it; a welcome change from the horse smells of the city and the coal smoke of the train station. The garden gave off a marvelous mixed odor of growing things. As I wandered through rows of corn beginning to ear out, the broad leaves slithered across my shirtsleeves and seemed to whisper, "Welcome, Casey, welcome." Just beyond were dozens of tomato plants. I'd seldom eaten tomatoes. Now I saw hundreds of them, as big as my fist and beginning to turn red . . . soon to be ready for the table.

Next to the tomatoes were dark green bushes. Some had been dug up. I knelt down and ran my fingers through the dirt. What a happy find! I uncovered a small red potato. Now I knew where the delicious buttered potatoes that had been on my dinner plate came from. A bit further on, I noticed two long rows of tiny plants with the imprint of someone's knees in the soft earth next to the green sprouts. With closer look, I recognized tiny carrots, pulled out and left by the side.

At the far end of the row, I spotted something even more interesting than vegetables . . . a person facing the other way on hands and knees.

I thought, "How can I approach this gardener without startling him?"

I knelt and picked up a stick, snapped it in two, and scratched in the dirt, looking for another potato. The sharp sound did the trick. The person stopped and turned around. It was a girl of about 12 or 13. She got to her feet and swayed a bit.

"Hello, I'll bet you're Casey Jones."

"Yes. Are you one of my cousins?"

"Yes, I've heard about you, and I think it's funny you have the same name as that engineer who wrecked his train."

I thought, "There we go, the engineer thing again."

I said, "Funny? A train wreck?"

"I don't mean funny ha-ha. I mean funny strange."

I liked this girl right off. She wore denim pants and a loose, blue, sleeveless top. Her tanned face looked up at me with big brown eyes from under a floppy yellow hat, and her smile sparkled as she looked me over.

I got the urge to tease.

"Well, I'm sure your name isn't funny or strange either."

"Why?"

I took a step forward and gazed at her. "Well, a good-looking girl like you must have a pretty name, like Natalie, Sophia or maybe even Annabell."

Annabell's mouth opened in surprise.

"Sally told you!"

"In a way she did, I heard your mother asking Sally your whereabouts." I smiled. "Annabell, under your smooth tan, I'll bet you're blushing."

"So you came out here to tease me."

"I apologize. I really didn't come out to find you, and teasing was just an impulse."

Annabell took off her hat and wiped her face with her arm.

I quickly added, "I'm sorry. I really should have said that you have a wonderful garden. I'm from the city, where we don't have gardens. I'm impressed."

Annabell's smile returned, so I went on.

"Just now I happened on the potatoes and I realized that I'd had some of those tasty little reds as part of my first meal here. Ummm. Delicious."

Annabell put her hat back on and gazed at me.

"I'm the one who should say I'm sorry. I should have given you a better welcome. Have you met Colette?"

"Yes."

"I'll bet she gave you a really nice welcome."

"Nice enough. But you needn't be sorry for anything, and I like being here." I hurried on.

"Please, cousin Annabell, tell me why you're pulling up carrots?"

She squinted up at me. "You really are a city boy, aren't you? Carrot seeds are small and fine. The only way to plant them is close together. When they sprout, they need to be thinned out so they'll have room to grow."

"Now that you've told me, it's obvious. Guess I have a lot to learn."

Annabell continued to stare at me, maybe to see if I was teasing again.

"Do you want some advice?"

"Please. I need it."

"Well, before you go anywhere, you'd better get out of those pants."

Now it was my turn to show surprise.

"Pants! What do you mean?"

Annabell turned back to her gardening. "I need to finish the carrots before I get cleaned up for supper. . ." As I walked off, I heard her say, "...and I go by Annie."

Strolling back, I felt cheerful enough to hum a tune: "Oh Susanna! Don't you cry for me."

I stepped around a tool shed. "I come from Alabama with a banjo on my knee. . ." suddenly a heavy blow to my shoulder spun me around to receive a heavy kick in the lower stomach. The pain was almost unbearable. Knees up, I fell, face forward.

A young man's voice, in low tones only I would hear, growled, "You look so stupid in those sissy pants! Go ahead. Eat dirt!" I felt his shoe on the back of my head as he pushed my face into the soft earth. By the time I recovered enough to look up, I was alone.

"Vernon!" I thought. The homesickness I'd been warding off for days flooded over me like filthy run-off from the gutter. Now, deeply depressed, back in my room, I paced back and forth, walking off the pain in my belly; I had to contend with sheer panic. What could make me more miserable than a kick in the groin? Then I thought, "I'll bet Dad's appendicitis hurt him even more."

Pants? Annie warned me about my pants. Now, worse than that, Vernon had ridiculed me about them too.

I only had two pairs of pants and they were the same. In New York, all the boys wore them. They're called knickers; cut short at mid-calf and bloused with a knitted cuff, British style. Socks were pulled up to meet them. I went to the window at the end of the hall and looked out on the street. Several boys walked by as I watched. None wore knickers.

four

THE KINSMAN CLAN

ANNIE

The evening meal was served in Overton Manor's large dining room. The whole family was there. I met another cousin who greeted me from across the table. "Hello, Casey," she said cheerfully. "I'm Neva. In case you're wondering, I'm fifteen. I'll be a junior in high school next term."

Mrs. Kinsman spoke up. "And Casey, this my sister, Olga Boltus."

I looked down the table at a woman dressed in black. "This is Casey Jones, Olga. We're pleased to have another member of the family staying with us."

I responded with, "How do you do, Mrs. Boltus."

Olga Boltus seemed unfriendly. She nodded in my direction and quickly turned her eyes away.

Mrs. Kinsman went on: "You still haven't met Olga's son, who lives across town. He has his own apartment now. His name is Vernon."

Vernon! My inner voice shouted, "My God! I've met him! Don't I have a stomach ache to prove it?"

Aunt Olga didn't say a word during dinner and left the table early, but the rest of us had a very pleasant chat. Everyone kept me busy answering questions about New York.

"I've seen pictures of the tall buildings, Casey. Have you been up in any of them?" Neva asked.

"The Manhattan Eye and Ear Clinic is about twenty stories, but I wasn't able to enjoy the view from the top floor. I had to go there because, while I was chopping a piece of wood, it flipped up and hit me in the face. That day, a Dr. Kenyon took a dozen slivers out of my eye."

"Who plays that piano I saw in the parlor?" I asked, eager to change the subject.

Neva smiled. "I do some. Mom gives me piano lessons. She is the pianist in the family."

Mrs. Kinsman smiled. "After dinner we sometimes have a little music, Casey. Maybe we can talk Neva into playing for us when we finish dessert."

Colette chimed in with, "Do you play?"

"Not the piano."

"That sounds like you might play some other instrument."

I mentally kicked myself for inviting that question.

"Well, I have played some on the mandolin."

"Mandolin? Is that anything like a guitar?" asked Annie.

"I've wanted to see about that. Do you have a guitar here."

Colette bounced on her chair. "Yes. You'll get a chance to find out."

As promised, Neva gave us several really lively piano pieces as we sat around the music room. Then everyone looked at me as Colette brought out a beautifully made guitar and handed it to Neva, who tuned it up before passing it to me.

I found, after testing it out, that I could play simple chords for a few numbers I'd learned from our neighbor, Mr. Lambrusco. I finished with a number called Valencia! I was surprised at how enthusiastically the family received my playing. I was too shy to try singing along.

Mr. Kinsman summed it up: "Casey, except in church, we don't hear much music way out west here. It's so refreshing to hear the guitar played so well. Thank you and be ready . . . rest assured you'll be called on again."

Then the man of the house went on: "Now Casey, you've met most of the family, but not Lobo. He's the family dog."

Colette lit up: "Oh Casey, you're going to love Lobo. That's Spanish for wolf, and his mother was a wolf. Lobo's father was our big dog on the ranch before a cougar killed him. Now Lobo's taken his place. Lobo's just the smartest and best dog any family could ever have!"

As I listened carefully to this dog and ranch talk, it hit me. I had become a part of this family. Life here was fast paced and I was caught up in the middle of it.

"Colette gets a little carried away when it comes to the dog, Casey," Mr. Kinsman continued. "But what she says is true. Lobo is an extraordinary animal; you'll find out for yourself when the girls take you out to the ranch this evening."

"Today?" all the girls said at once.

Neva spoke up. "Daddy, are you going to let us drive Casey out there right now?"

"Yes. I've got the buckboard wagon with the horse all harnessed up for you. Be prepared to spend the night."

Annie jumped up and shouted. "C'mon. Let's change into our cov'ralls!

The others shouted, "Yes!"

I loved the excitement of the moment as the cousins happily hopped up and headed for the stairs.

Mrs. Kinsman laughed at their exuberance then turned to me. "Casey, we should explain that Overton Manor is our residence here in town. The ranch is our home in the country."

Mr. Kinsman got up to go. "I must excuse myself, Casey.

I have a pile of paperwork waiting in my office down at the depot. You see, I'm the Northern Pacific Railroad's Superintendent for this Western Division. The girls will take good care of you, as will Bernie Wellman and his wife, Stella. They are the caretakers at our ranch that we've named K2."

"I'm sure looking forward to seeing your country home, Mr. Kinsman." Then I blurted out, "And maybe some time, I can visit your office too."

Mr. Kinsman paused and gave his wife a knowing look. "Yes, Casey. You'll see my office in good time. But for the next few days, you might learn the ABCs of the K2 Ranch."

"I will." Again I spoke impulsively. "Excuse me, sir. "May I please call you Uncle Harry?"

"I want you to," he replied.

Mrs. Kinsman then took her cue to respond in kind. "And you must call me Aunt Louise."

five

A BRUSH WITH DEATH

NEVA

I hadn't unpacked my bag, so it was easy just to pick it up and get set to go out to the ranch. Sally led me to a comfortable chair by the back door.

"You got ready quickly, Casey," she said. "But, with the girls so eager to get out to K2, they won't keep you waiting long."

Sally was right. Neva appeared first with a little overnight bag of her personal things. She plopped down next to me and smiled a question. "Well, Casey, what do you think of us so far?

"Neva, you are flat out the finest folks a fella could have. I can't fully fathom it. I've been here only a few hours. Yet, in some ways I feel like it's been all my life."

"Casey, I know I speak for all of us and feel the same about you. You really fit in."

"Thanks, Neva. But I have one big question."

"Stop! I know what it is, and we're not supposed to talk with you about it until after you've been with us a bit longer. Please be patient."

We hadn't mentioned his name, but Neva and I both knew that Vernon posed a problem. I sensed something sinister about both Vernon and his mother, Mrs. Boltus.

"O. K., I trust you, Neva. My question will wait."

As we heard Annie and Colette on the stairs, Neva jumped up. "Let's go, Casey." Neva tossed her head and laughed, "Unless you're too shy to ride with three girls all by yourself."

"Not on your life!" I laughed, and ran out to the one-horse wagon.

Neva, on the front seat, called out, "Casey, ride up here with me."

With a slap of the reins and a "giddap!" from Neva, our wagon set off down the winding driveway. Soon the four of us were happily chattering away as we wheeled out onto a country road, with the summer sun low in the sky.

On the outside I was all smiles and chuckles as I responded to my cousins' cute comments. But inside I couldn't dismiss a worrisome thought: I'm in some sort of danger and these kind folks are shielding me; getting me out of town.

The Arborville countryside was rich farmland, no sagebrush in sight. When we came to the K2 Ranch, dark green fields rolled by. "That's alfalfa," said Neva.

Colette chirped, "Casey, those beautiful grassy fields up ahead are barley. See how they're beginning to get plump heads with whiskers on the stems. Barley is a good crop to grow out here because it brings a nice price per bushel and doesn't need to be irrigated, like the alfalfa does. It's a dry-land crop."

"Then why raise alfalfa?"

"Because we need hay for the cattle."

Annie gave me a sideways smile. "Be truthful now, Casey. Did you know that alfalfa is hay?"

My face got red. "I've never had to give it a thought."

This brought giggles from all three girls.

"You've got a lot to learn." sighed Colette, as she flashed her green eyes at me.

"Your dad said I should learn the ABCs of this ranch. Looks

like that means alfalfa, barley and cattle."

All three girls burst out laughing.

Neva, still holding the reins, gave me an admiring look. "Casey! That's clever! Come to think of it, that's exactly what Dad wants you to do. I'd never pinned it down the ABCs of K2 that way."

"Colette, you mentioned that the alfalfa is irrigated. How?"

"There's a network of canals that brings water down from a dam on the Serpentine River." Colette answered.

"Where's the nearest canal?"

Neva pointed to a distant dwelling. "The K2 ranch house is over there. The canal's a short hike beyond the barn. A series of ditches control the flow into the fields."

We arrived a good hour before sundown. The wagon stopped in front of a rambling one-story wood frame farmhouse with a tile roof and a huge gray barn in back. A white rail fence extended back beyond a neat lawn studded with shrubs and a row of tall, poplar shade trees that followed the curved driveway up to the front door. I thought to myself, "What a beautiful place!"

A farm-hand took charge of the horse and wagon, and we strolled over to where Bernie and Stella Wellman were waiting with a warm welcome.

Before the girls could introduce me, Bernie stepped forward. "You must be Casey Jones. Pleased to meet you, Casey. You have a famous name. Any relation to the engineer?"

"No, Mr. Wellman. Jones is a common name."

"Call me Bernie."

Mrs. Wellman stepped forward: "Welcome, Casey, and call me Stella. Make yourself at home now while you're here. I'll show you to your room."

The girls went to their rooms and, for the second time in

one day, I was looking around a bedroom intended for my use. I liked this one too. It had a sliding, glass door that opened out to the pretty yard, where bright orange and yellow mums and marigolds bloomed. I could see all the way to the blue-gray hills in the distance.

I wandered out through the living room, furnished with western style furniture and colorful tapestries, to the kitchen, where I found Stella using a wooden barrel-like device that, she explained, was used to churn cream into butter.

"Stella, I've never been on a farm before. If it's O.K., I'm going to take a quick look around."

She nodded, and I headed out the back door, past the barn and across an alfalfa field to what looked like the banks that sloped up to an irrigation canal. Yes! I soon stood on the edge and leaned over, looking down at the swiftly moving stream of ditch water, some twelve feet across. It seemed fairly deep.

Just then, I was startled by the loud, menacing, bark of a dog. As I quickly straightened up, I lost my balance. The moss on the ditch bank was slippery. I slid and grabbed frantically at some tall grass, but still went in with a splash.

Cold water assaulted my skin, shot up my nose, and my mind reeled: "City Boy! You dumb City Boy! Never learned to swim! CAN'T TOUCH BOTTOM! Now you're in for it! Help me dear God! Help me get out of here! Can't hold my breath much longer! MOVE ARMS! KICK! GET TO SURFACE!

THANK GOD! I popped to the surface for a second, just long enough to gulp some air and get a mouthful of water too as the swirling current pulled me under again and swept me down the ditch. Going to DROWN!

MY SHOULDER HIT A BRANCH OR SOMETHING. It jammed into my shirt in back. IT'S PUSHING ME TO THE SURFACE!

AIR! AIR! I CAN BREATHE! I'm not sinking. SOME-

ONE'S PUSHING ME OVER TO THE BANK... HOLDING ME AGAINST IT!

DUMMY! QUICK, GRAB SOMETHING! A SHRUB! YES! Slowly now! Climb up the slippery slope."

I got a boost from behind! WHO? WHAT?

It's a DOG! A HUGE DOG!

Scramble up. Roll over. Get your breath.

Thank God! THANK YOU! I'm not going to drown in a ditch. I'm not going to ... die.

As I lay there shaking all over, gasping, the big shaggy dog came up beside me. He growled a threatening, RARRRAAHH, and then gave out two of those deafeningly loud barks, like the one that startled me into falling.

With lips curled back the dog snapped his teeth. I sensed someone else by the ditch bank. I reared up on one elbow; my vision cleared.

Vernon with his same look of hatred, sneered down at me. The dog seemed to be protecting me from Vernon. Yes! Except for the dog, Vernon might have TRIED TO PUSH ME BACK IN.

I rolled down the embankment away from the water, then slowly rose to my feet facing Vernon.

He spoke first. "You stupid, dumb, jackass of a kid! The first time you get on a farm with no girls around to baby you, and what happens? You fall in a ditch and almost drown! You must have cow dung for brains! If the dog hadn't pulled you out, you'd be buzzard bait! GET OUT! GO ON TO SEATTLE OR GET KILLED!" Vernon's eyes were blazing and he punched the air with his fists.

"GET OUT! YOU HEAR ME? YOU DON'T BELONG HERE!"

Vernon stalked down the slope and disappeared. Seconds later I heard a horse gallop off.

Vernon's verbal abuse hit as hard as had his earlier kick in the stomach. I slumped down, wet head in my hands, shaking with misery, almost sorry I'd survived. I felt like . . .when . . .

For a few seconds I re-lived coming home from Dad's funeral with Mom, trying to hold back the tears as we walked back to our cold apartment.

I sobbed, "Oh Dad, I wish you were with me now!" Then I raised up, fighting off the dreary mood.

The dog shook himself and snorted. With his wolf-like stand-up ears and beautiful tawny coat, he stood panting; looking at me with an almost human expression of friendliness. He seemed to say, "C'mon Casey, things aren't so bad. You're alive and the folks back at the house like you."

Then I noticed the bluish eyes. "Lobo? Are you Lobo?"

Several quick wags of his tail seemed to answer, yes. He turned and trotted toward the ranch house. I followed him back, silently slipping through the sliding door to my room.

Following a shower and with dry clothes, I sauntered out into the living room as though nothing had happened. But my heart still tripped like a tom-tom.

six

WOLF BLOOD ON GUARD

COLETTE

I couldn't be certain that no one here had observed my close call in the ditch. But it didn't come up when we got together for milk and cookies, so I relaxed and joined in the girls' banter.

The Wellmans were treated as family. After Stella placed the simple refreshments on the table, she sat down and poured coffee for Bernie and herself.

"What do you think of our K2 ranch so far, Casey?" She asked.

"Compared to all that sage-brush country I saw this morning, it's almost too good to be true. I hope to learn all about this fine farm."

Everyone smiled at my answer, then I enjoyed hearing first one, then another of the girls giving me sage advice. They could hardly wait for tomorrow; their pretty, bright faces shone with anticipation.

Neva pushed an amber curl from her face as she explained, "We're going to have to get back to town after lunch tomorrow, Casey. But we'll have all morning to show you around."

Annie beamed as she added, "Yes, and that means no sleeping in. We need to get up early and make the most of the morning."

Neva's serious expression helped make the point. "Casey, we don't want to overdo it, but tomorrow we should make every minute count."

I was exhausted after the most eventful day of my life. It seemed more like a week ago, but it was just this morning when I woke up on the train. Then, when I got off, my life actually speeded up to the wild gallop of a runaway horse.

Now, I fought to stay awake as the girls joyfully planned the next day.

I heard Neva say, "We can take Casey in the buckboard out to see the far pasture where the Hereford cattle are grazing."

"Good idea," Colette replied. "Then we can head over to Funnel Creek. There're deer up in the canyon. We might see 'em."

"O.K.," agreed Bernie. "But we should circle back around to check out the wooded area that follows the creek. I've seen several coveys of quail in there recently. And we should take the .22 rifle along too, in case we stir up a few rabbits."

Stella liked that idea. "Good. We could have rabbit for dinner tomorrow."

I roused up. "Rabbit for dinner? Are you serious?" I asked.

Everyone smiled at me. Neva gave me another sideways look. "Now, Casey. I'll bet you're going to tell us that you've never eaten rabbit."

I paused and looked at everybody's expression to see if they were kidding me. I decided they weren't. "I guess there's a lot of things I've not tried."

Neva went on. "You'll like rabbit. It tastes like chicken."

Back in my room, I tossed pants and shirt aside. I was exhausted. Just as I flopped on the bed, I heard the sound of soft steps coming toward me.

Heart pounding, I peered into the gloom expecting to see a menacing Vernon about to pounce on me.

Then I heard a loud snuff, as Lobo blew dust from his nose. He'd come to spend the night and protect me.

Never had I heard such a reassuring sound. I grabbed a handful of his soft coat and drew him to me. Lobo, in turn, put a big paw on the bed. For a full minute I hugged him, and he licked my ear. Sheer relief poured out, and I cried tears of love for my new animal friend. I'd tried to put up an inner wall of strength. Now I had Lobo to help me meet Vernon's awful challenge.

"Lobo! Lobo," I whispered, as love welled up in my heart. "You're an answer to a prayer! With you by my side, I'll be safe tonight."

seven

MISSING LOBO

CHIN LEE
AND JASPER

Hours later I struggled to come out of a dreamless sleep. My comfortable bed was like sleeping nestled in a warm cloud. As I tried to get fully awake, thoughts of train stations and country roads swirled around in my head. It seemed like I'd stepped through Alice's looking glass. The big rabbit in the story had better not come by. The folks here might eat him!

Sunshine streamed in through the sliding door as Stella pulled the drape aside.

"Good morning, young man," she said cheerfully. "You'd want to sleep 'til noon, but those cousins of yours are a chompin' at the bit; rearin' to go."

Lobo was gone. Had I dreamed that he'd come to me?

"It's nigh on nine o'clock. That's late on the farm. You'll have to grab a quick bowl o' mush and get with the day! Bernie's talkin' about putting our hired hand, Chin Lee, in charge of teaching you to ride. There's a nice little pony named Jasper picked out for you."

Stella had found some shirts and pants my size . . . all clean, starched, and very welcome. Decked out in them, I felt less an easterner; a point made by Neva as she looked up from the kitchen table.

"Well, mornin' Casey. If you top off your frame with a cowboy hat, you might fool folks into thinking you're from around here." Annie piped up and shook her head. "Nooo, there's still too much dude in his walk and talk to fool anybody."

Colette looked me up and down with a wan smile. "You can take the boy outa the city but you can't take the city outa the boy."

Cheered up by my pretty cousins, I needed to reply, but later on I was to regret what I blurted out.

"Well, my cousins," I began. "We'll just see about that. I may not have mastered the western swagger by the time you get out here again, but I intend to be riding a horse all over the place by then."

Bernie snorted. "How long do you think these gals are goin' to stay in town, a month?"

Red-faced, I changed the subject as everyone laughed at Bernie's comment.

"Well, we'll see. And for now I'll settle for a bowl of mush."

Instantly Stella served me with a steaming bowl of oatmeal and raisins, and I poured cream over it all.

"Brown sugar?" she offered, pushing the bowl across the table to me.

I answered her with an expression I'd heard from Bernie. "Thank ye kindly, Ma'am," which broke up the table in laughter.

Annie grinned, "Drawled like a true cow-poke, Casey."

On the way out to the wagon, Bernie handed me a broad-brimmed hat. "Here, if this don't fit just right, I've another you can use."

The hat fit perfectly. I loved the growing westernized feel of things.

Minutes later, we clamored into the buckboard and, after viewing over five hundred head of fine, healthy-looking cattle, circled back by way of Funnel Creek. It had been a fun morning. I had seen my first deer at a distance and, at one point, I was surprised to see Annie jump out, raise a .22 rifle and bag two rabbits. I admired her skill.

When we arrived back, a bit dusty and weary, Stella met us at the back door. "Have you seen Lobo? He didn't show up for his morning meal."

Bernie looked worried. "That's not like him. That dog is as regular and dependable in his habits as a mailman."

I could tell the girls were worried too.

Annie said for everybody. "Golly, I sure hope he's not lying sick somewhere."

Bernie stood thoughtfully, stroking his chin. "No point in lookin' for him. There's a thousand places where he could be. We'll just have to wait and hope he comes back to us."

I was torn at that point between telling about Lobo saving my life, or just waiting to see if he came back. After all, last night he'd stretched out by my bed. The nagging question was, did Vernon have anything to do with Lobo's disappearance?

During lunch, the girls didn't seem to be talking about anything in particular. But as we finished, I sensed that a pre-arranged comment had surfaced.

The girls climbed into the buckboard with Neva in the driver's seat. Annie took up the challenge. "We'll be back in just three days, Casey. Maybe you can ride out to meet us on Jasper."

I could hardly wait for the girls to leave. Out of the corner of my eye, I saw Bernie walking out of the barn with a young man leading a horse, and I jogged over to them.

"Casey, this is Chin Lee." We shook hands, and Chin Lee smiled and nodded. "He's gonna give you a bit of training so's you can get up and ride Jasper here."

Jasper snorted and wagged his head as though to say: "Oh, no you're not."

"Casey," Chin Lee began. "Approach Jasper from the left side and get his reins in your hand before you mount. Then put your foot in the stirrup and swing your leg over as you come up, like this." I watched Chin Lee rise up smoothly and slide into the saddle. It looked easy, but what happened next was so awful I try to block it out of my mind.

eight

JOUSTING WITH JASPER

That night I wrote a letter to my mom. In a few words I described how Uncle Harry had found me on the railroad platform and told me about the change in plans. He brought me to Overton Manor and introduced me to the family. Then I told her of the Kinsman ranch and offered my guess that I'd be living here for a while. I wanted to be mostly upbeat about things, so I didn't mention Vernon or Lobo. When I came to Jasper, I provided some details.

"Looking back on it, Mom, I was really over-eager to show everybody I could learn to ride this horse named Jasper.

"Chin Lee is the hand who will teach me to ride.

"Mom, I watched Chin Lee rise up and slide into the saddle. It looked so easy, but what happened next was awful.

"The first time I hoisted myself up into the saddle, Jasper first moved away from me a bit, and then, as I swung my leg over, he stopped his sideways motion. This caused me to tip toward the other side of him. I slid across the saddle, my foot came out of the stirrup, and I crashed to the ground on the far side.

"Mom, I was crushed. Lying there in the dust with everybody whooping it up, laughing like it was the funniest thing they'd ever seen. Talk about a greenhorn from New York! It's a good thing I wasn't wearing my knickers! I jumped up to try again.

"I forgot everything I'd been told. I rushed it. Trying again, I was on the other side of the horse, so when I put my foot in the stirrup and swung my leg over, this time I came down backwards in the saddle and with the reins dragging on the ground behind me.

"Jasper happily trotted about, giving the onlookers a close-up view of my 'trial by horse.' For those watching, it must have seemed like something from a Wild West Show comedy as I wildly bounced around, hanging onto Jasper's tail.

"How to end it? I managed to swing one arm around and grasp the saddle pommel to keep from falling off again . . . this time from a moving horse.

"Then as I rode sideways, still clutching Jasper's tail with one hand, he took another turn around the paddock. I thought, 'This has turned into a circus act, with me as the clown.'

"More ranch hands joined the onlookers shouting and yelling. They slapped their knees laughing at the sight of a New Yorker gyrating on a tame cowpony. Would I ever live it down?

"Chin Lee jumped on his horse and caught up to Jasper and me. He grabbed the reins and brought us to a gentle stop; his arm steadied me as I swung back around .

"'Get both feet in the stirrups, Casey; take the reins and hold back on them gently until you're ready to go.'

"Mom, what a great relief it was to get set up right! Chin Lee talked me into just the right set of actions and within minutes the laughter stopped as our horses began to move, side by side, in a large circle. After a few minutes, Chin Lee moved away and Jasper and I went on.

"'Grip with your legs; move the reins from side to side. See how Jasper responds to those movements; you don't even have to say 'gee' or 'haw' for him know you want him to turn one way or the other, that's for plow horses.'

"I noticed that with the reins loosened, Jasper began to trot. I pushed down in the stirrups to keep from bouncing. I tried to anticipate his rhythm and it worked.

"Chin Lee cautioned me: 'Careful not to bump Jasper's flanks with your heels, Casey. He might take that as a signal for him to break into a gallop.'

"At that point, I sure didn't want Jasper to go any faster!

"'If he does speed up, just pull back gently on the reins and say, "whoa!"'

"At that moment, Jasper heard that command to stop, and that's what he did . . . causing me to clutch the pommel frantically to avoid leaving the saddle head-first. This created another round of whooping laughter. "I leaned forward loosening the reins and whispered, 'Let's go, Jasper.' "This time Jasper cooperated with a slow trot around the paddock. Then I reined him to a stop with a 'Whoa, boy.'

"We came to a gentle stop. This was the moment I needed to convince all the onlookers that I was determined to get on with things at K2. On an impulse, I stood up in the stirrups, pulled off my cowboy hat, and used it to make a sweeping motion to those assembled. I smiled and bowed low. Everyone loved the gesture and a several clapped their hands. The show was over.

"Mom, I heard someone say, 'The kid's got grit!'

"Not to push my luck, I quickly threw my leg over and slipped to the ground. I thanked God that the first big challenge of K2 Ranch was over. And Mom, I sensed that it was not just a test in the art of horsemanship, but also an answer to the question of acceptance by the fine folks on the K2 Ranch.

"For a long moment I stood patting Jasper on the neck. In

low-pitched tones I offered up words of thanks for reaching a point where I might prove Vernon wrong. 'With your help, Dear God . . . with Your help, I'll do it.'

"Just then, Mom, I heard Chin Lee at my side. He took it that I'd been talking to the horse. 'Good idea to talk to him that way, Casey. He wants to be your friend, and needs to know that you want his friendship too.'

"I hope that things are going well with you in New York, Mom. I miss you and look forward to getting a letter from you."

I signed it and added two postscripts.

"P.S. Please send my regrets to Aunt Minnie for not being able to take her up on the offer to live with her and help out in the fish market. I was looking forward to going to Seattle.

"P.P.S. Say hi to Mr. Lambrusco for me. Tell him that, thanks to his mandolin lessons, I can play a few chords on the guitar."

nine

LOBO ON THE TRAIL   CAL PALUSKIN

*L*ater that day, I watched Chin Lee ride in from the North 80 cattle area. Horse and rider were as one. Both stopped and Chin Lee dismounted, all in one smooth movement. My first attempt in the saddle had been an embarrassment. How hilarious for the farm hands! But the Greenhorn hadn't given up. I was spurred on to get the hang of horsemanship.

I watched others as they used feet and legs to guide the rhythm of riding.

I made learning to saddle up and ride my top priority. Chin Lee helped me for the rest of the afternoon as we rode back and forth on the front road.

From early morning on the second day, I put Jasper through a series of riding sessions, until I felt ready to head out and look around for Lobo. It had been 24 hours since he'd disappeared. I could sense that Bernie and the others were starting to give up on him.

When I mentioned Lobo to Bernie, he stared at me before answering.

"Son, animals on a farm come and go. Lobo was one of the

best, but we'll just have to own up to the fact that he's gone."

"I'm not quite ready to accept that." I replied. "I need to practice learning to ride. Is it O.K. if I take Jasper?"

"Jasper is yours to use while you're here. Be sure he's fed before you leave, and curry him down when you get back."

I swung through the kitchen on my way out. Stella handed me a rucksack with lunch and something else I'd only heard about, a canteen of water that slid easily into my saddlebag.

Despite the rough start, I'd picked up some fine points of riding. I needed a boost to my morale right now. Eager to try out my new skills, I rode Jasper out through the paddock, down the road, and headed toward higher ground. Secure in the saddle, I thought: "Casey, you just might be a natural for this. After all, your mother was born and raised out here. I'm a westerner who has come home to live. Let Vernon do his worst. I'm sticking with this life!"

We loped along for ten minutes and arrived at a rise that gave me a panoramic view of K2.

"Whoa, Jasper. We've got to figure out where our friend Lobo might be. I've got to think like him."

I could see the main buildings down below, and the fields that spread out from them to the north and east.

"Jasper, you live here. What would prompt Lobo to leave the Ranch and barn area? Maybe he left my room to check out an intruder! I'll bet that's it! As I slept in, Lobo was on duty. He picked up on Vernon's return visit in the early morning and went out to confront him."

By coincidence, Jasper whinnied, nodding his head up and down as if in agreement.

As I pondered the question of where they might have met, I let my eyes travel the main road into K2. Vernon would be on horseback. Like yesterday, he probably left the road and followed the canal trail, a shortcut to the ranch house. If true,

Lobo could have intercepted him somewhere along the row of poplar trees.

I set Jasper to a gallop. About a half-mile up from the main house, I reined in.

"O.K. now, fella, let's slow it up and have a look around."

Colette had mentioned yesterday that this long row of tall trees served a purpose as a windbreak that ran between the fields following a ditch from the main canal. Around the trunks of the poplars grew thorny locust mingled with brush, providing habitat for rabbits and other small animals. It occurred to me that if a rider left a horse tethered back a ways, he could lie in wait alongside the trail in this brushy area, ready to ambush a traveler.

I slid off Jasper. Reins in hand, I led him on the windbreak trail.

Just then, a high-pitched whine came from off to the left. Jasper whinnied and gave a throaty sound in response. We both stood still, not breathing for several seconds while I scanned the tangled embankment.

At first, nothing. Then, a closer look at the hard-packed trail brought out something unusual; scratches in the dirt, signs of a skirmish. I noticed broken branches near the ditch. My heart began to pound as I peered over and down to the water's edge. There, covered with blood, with his battered head near the water, lay my fine, loving friend, Lobo.

My tears burst forth as I knelt and reached out to him. Matted hair covered numerous wounds and welts all about his head, neck and shoulders. He'd been badly beaten and then left for dead. But he had held on, waiting for us to find him. Flies buzzed around his wounds and one of his beautiful blue eyes was swollen shut, encrusted and scabbed over with blood. He'd dragged himself to water and had kept himself alive as his heart refused to stop.

"Lobo! Lobo," I sobbed. "Please live! I love you, big Bo!"

And Lobo heard me, responding with a slight wag and thump of his muddy tail.

I vowed I'd do anything to nurse him. Muttering soothing sounds to him, I jerked off my bandanna, moistened it and dabbed at his wounds. I leaned over and checked out his other eye. It was slightly swollen but the right side of Lobo's head was hardly injured. "Thank God for that!" I said earnestly. As I tried to comfort this amazing animal, I prayed. Oh! How I prayed! Not even when my dad was having his appendicitis operation had I prayed harder.

As I washed the caked blood from his wounds, I could see that some were infected. He was still alive, but unless he got some good attention soon, I knew Lobo would surely die.

Lobo had come into my life only two days ago and yet I felt a closeness, a bond of love with him. With his good eye, Lobo looked up at me with such gratitude that I had to put my head down, racked by sobbing. Love for this animal mixed with loathing for the one who had done this evil thing. Vernon's smooth face, contorted with hatred, filled my inner vision.

I talked myself back to reason. "Keep helping him but THINK! What are you going to do next? He needs help. Dear God, help me to help him."

I scrambled to my feet. Lobo lay in the shade and had water to drink. There was nothing more I could do for him here. Before I rode the half-mile to the house for help, I climbed into the crotch of a poplar tree and shaded my eyes against the sun . . . searching for someone to help.

Yes! On the driveway from the house, a ranch hand was riding swiftly out toward town. I scrambled through the brush, mounted Jasper, and was on my way to the rider.

Minutes later, I intercepted Cal Paluskin, a ranch hand I'd met before. On the way back to the injured dog, I told him about Lobo. Cal pulled a container of salve from his saddlebag and continued the washing of Lobo's wounds that I'd begun. Then he smeared generous amounts of the salve on each affected area. I watched, gaining hope for Lobo's recovery from Cal's sure-handed manner. I thought, "Cal has tended wounded animals before." Was it just by chance I found him out there just now? He seemed an answer to a prayer.

Cal looked at me. "We must turn him over." He spread a blanket beside the dog and between the two of us, in one motion, we rolled the big dog onto it and turned him over. The process of washing and salving the wounds was repeated on the other side.

"What kind of salve are you using, Cal?"

"Bear grease and herbs. It will help heal him."

"Bear grease? Are you sure?"

"Yes, shot the big brown up on the ridge before he could stir up the herd."

"Oh," I said mildly. Protecting the herd. Reason enough for Bernie to hire Cal.

"The dog should live." Cal said flatly. "You know who beat him up this way?"

A seething rage at Vernon surfaced. I turned my head away. I was sure my face was turning red. Mr. Lambrusco once told me of a steward on the steamship that had brought him to New York. For eleven days the man had used his position to shout obscenities at the men and women who were packed together in the lower deck. Hungry and mistreated, Mr. Lambrusco told of his hatred for the man that built each day of the voyage. But as they steamed into New York harbor, a priest traveling with them counseled everyone: "Control your hatred. We are entering a new life. Don't begin it with bad feelings that will hurt only those who hold on to them."

Now I was the one with hatred in my heart. Would I allow

it to poison me?

So, "Maybe," was my cryptic reply to Cal.

"Umm. You don't want to tell me."

"Would you put the blame of something bad as this on a man if you didn't know for sure."

"You speak wisely for one so young. But since I came to work here for Bernie five years ago, Lobo has been my friend, I have a stake in this."

I trusted Cal. "I need help not only for Lobo, but for myself too. I'll tell you what I know."

In a few words I told Cal some of Vernon's threats against me, omitting the attack in the Overton garden, but including the episode after Lobo saved me from drowning in the canal.

Cal leaned against a tree trunk. While he had gently tended to Lobo with his native medicine, I hadn't realized his fierce inner strength. The muscles on his bronze arms tightened and his dark eyes narrowed.

"Uhunh," he grunted. "You and Lobo need a friend."

"Thanks, Cal." Our eyes met. "Believe me, I appreciate your offer to help."

Cal closed his eyes for a few seconds, then quickly detailed a plan of action.

"Next time you see Mr. Kinsman, tell him Vernon makes war on you. Tell Bernie too, but they must let you work it out. I will care for Lobo . . . you can help. No one else should know Lobo still lives. Let others think he's dead . . . maybe killed by a cougar like his father."

I felt my heart leap with joy at this turn of events. "Where are we going to keep Lobo?"

"I live in the bunkhouse with the other K2 hands," Cal replied. "But Bernie knows about my hideaway up on the hillside. I go there some to hunt. It is a place that has been used by family for many generations. Lobo will be safe at the hideaway. I'll show you how to get there."

I looked down on the wounded dog, asleep and breathing normally now.

"Cal," I asked, getting a little choked up, "is Lobo going to fully heal, get back to being the way he used to be?"

"Maybe." Cal replied. "I see no broken bones, just cracked ribs . . . and that's good. But he has some sickness inside that might not heal all the way."

At this I stifled a sob, but I sensed that if anyone could bring Lobo back to health, it would be Cal with his natural medicine of the woods.

Cal squinted at the sun. "Time for me to finish my job in town for Bernie. On my way back, I'll tend Lobo. Then after grub, I'll spend the rest of the night here. In early morning, I'll take him up to the hideaway."

"How will you do that? Can I help?"

"Travois best for him. Not bumpy like a wagon would be."

I'd seen a picture of a travois. Two long limbs were lashed together and fastened to a horse. Cal would tie his blanket, with Lobo on it, between the limbs whose far ends would simply drag on the trail behind. Perfect for Lobo!

Lobo didn't open his eyes as Cal checked on him. "He's resting now. That's good. Tonight I'll bring Lobo some venison broth I'll make from deer jerky. Maybe tomorrow he will begin to eat again.

"Have you eaten bear meat?" Cal asked.

"Bear meat? Cal, I'm from the city. I've never heard of eating bear meat."

"Uhunh. I will bring some to Stella to fix for you."

"Well, I don't know, Cal. I don't know if I could . . ."

"Bear grease is good medicine for dog wound, bear meat good medicine for spirit."

"W-well," I sputtered . . .

"Uhunh. You want dog to get well?"

"Yes, yes I do."

"Then you and I will eat bear meat. Lobo . . . you and I . . . we need the strength that comes from the mighty brown bear for the fight."

ten

UNCLE HARRY TRIES TO HELP

LOBO

As Jasper cantered along the windbreak, I thought of what I'd tell Bernie. I needed an explanation of the day's events.

Still a quarter of a mile from the ranch house, I pulled up. "Whoa, Jasper."

Consumed by thoughts of future challenges, I still enjoyed a small thrill at how quickly Jasper and I had gotten the feel of each other's thoughts and movements. Jasper was fast becoming my horse. As I led him to the ditch bank, I marveled at a wonder of nature. How quickly the human and animal bonds of spirit were intertwined . . . first with Lobo, and now with Jasper.

Hunger grabbed my attention. Jasper cropped tall grass and I sat on a cottonwood log, got out Stella's lunch, and soon took big bites from the sandwich she'd sent along.

Refreshed and feeling some better now that Lobo was being well cared for, Jasper and I continued back to the ranch house. Jasper knew that we were only minutes away from his stall in the barn. I gave him his head and, as we loped along, I took off my hat, enjoying the breeze ruffling my hair and the thrill of speeding across the fragrant fields. If it weren't for Vernon's campaign against me, I'd know inner peace. I loved this life in the open.

Eager to report in to Bernie, I still took time to care for Jasper as Chin Lee had taught me earlier.

Back in the stall, Jasper's horsy smell was pleasing to me. I purred, "Whoa, there, Jasper. I'll get your flanks combed down and then you'll be set. Tomorrow we'll get an early start for Cal's hideaway."

Startled by a voice from just behind me, I jumped around to face a smiling Neva.

"You're a fast learner, Casey. Good dressing down. I couldn't have done it better myself."

"Thanks, Neva. It's sure good to see you," I said, impulsively taking her hand. "When did you get here?"

"Just now. Dad sent me to get you in the Ford a day early. You'll be having the evening meal with us, then be back here by bedtime."

"Great! I really need someone friendly to talk to."

When I mentioned my plans for the rest of the day to Stella, she said, "I'll tell Bernie as soon as he gets in. Give my regards to Mr. and Mrs. Kinsman."

I quickly washed trail dust off, climbed into clean clothes, and again I thought, "Never a dull moment."

A minute later I was riding alongside Neva trying to catch her every word over the roar of the Ford's motor. It was a fast-paced life out here, but I enjoyed riding in a car, and I liked being with Neva.

"Dad wanted someone else in the family to learn how to drive this automobile." Neva explained. "Since Mom said flat out that she would never be comfortable behind the wheel of a car, I was happy to take Dad up on his offer to teach me to drive." Neva took a deep breath and then changed the subject.

"All right now, Casey. It's time to bring up Vernon." Neva gave me a serious sideways look. "By now, you must know that he has it in for you."

"Yes, he's made that clear." I decided not to mention the pushing and kicking incident in the garden, but I briefly described how I almost drowned in the canal, and how Lobo had saved my life there.

When I told of Vernon's threats and how Lobo seemed to protect me, Neva's eyes got big as she stared over the steering wheel.

"Casey!" She shouted over the sound of the Ford. "You're lucky to have survived! Even good swimmers have drowned in that canal!" After a minute of silence, she continued. "We sent you out of town to get you away from Vernon, but he followed you. Sorry about the trouble he's giving you."

"Neva, when I was talking to Jasper, did you hear me say where we were going tomorrow morning?"

"Yes, I heard you say 'the hideaway'. You make friends quickly, Casey. I'm really impressed. I know about Cal. He never invites anyone from K2 up to his hideaway. I don't know where it is. I'm really curious, why are you heading up there."

At this point I had to tell Neva about Lobo's being beaten and how Cal had tended to him.

"For his sake, I must ask you not to tell anyone that Lobo's still alive, recuperating at the hideaway."

"I'll keep the secret, Casey. But I'm shocked that Vernon would do such a mean and brutal thing! How sad . . . poor Lobo."

"I'm not positive that it was Vernon. But when Lobo saved me, I noticed Vernon glaring at him with clenched fists."

Neva's expression reflected anguish. "When his dad died a few years ago, Vernon and his mother came to live with us.

Dad wanted Vernon to learn all about railroading from the top down. We thought Vernon might begin to work with Dad and maybe actually take over a supervisory position, but it just wasn't working out. Dad gave him several chances to get it right, but Vernon would make mistakes, like when he sent a whole carload of potatoes to the wrong destination. They spoiled before the mistake could be corrected. Vernon didn't seem to care about railroading, and on the ranch he lorded it over everybody.

"It came as a shock when, two weeks ago, Dad asked him to leave. It didn't occur to Vernon that he'd lose his position. When he heard about you, another nephew, coming to live here, he went into a foaming rage."

Neva's description of Vernon's fall from favor and my being welcomed into the family didn't come as a complete surprise. I had suspected something like that from the first. Now I knew exactly why Vernon hated me.

Neva finished her amazing tale as we turned into the driveway. "Good timing" I thought. I'd been shocked into silence.

The afternoon sun filtered through Overton Manor's tall maple trees as we came to a stop. Annie and Colette ran to greet us.

"Casey," Annie shouted: "You've only been away two days, but we've missed you!"

Self-conscious at Annie's warm greeting, I laughed and gave her a little hug. "Thanks, Annie. There's a lot to do out at K2; it's good to get back here so's I can relax for an hour or two."

"I'll bet you've been learning to ride," guessed Colette.

"I have. Bernie has given me a horse named Jasper to use and I've been riding out and around quite a bit."

Annie observed, "I can tell, you're getting a cowboy's tan. Dark face and white neck where your bandanna's been."

We all laughed, and I hoped that maybe my new tan was

hiding my blushing.

At dinner, Mr. Kinsman led our prayer before the meal and, as we ate, everyone kept me busy telling about my K2 activities. I didn't mention my close call in the canal or Lobo's trouble. I did describe my embarrassing first ride on Jasper. This prompted a lot of laughter from everyone except Mrs. Boltus, who again left the table early.

After a delicious dessert of Aunt Louise's peach cobbler, Uncle Harry pushed aside his plate, picked up his coffee cup and said, "Casey, let's go into the next room. You and I need to talk."

We entered a wood-paneled room with numerous shelves filled with hundreds of books, a home library – the first of its kind I'd seen.

"These books can't all be about dry business," I thought. "I'll look them over first chance I get."

Uncle Harry motioned me into a comfortable chair as he began our chat.

"My grandfather Wil, an Arborville pioneer, invested heavily in railroads and cattle. With the help of my father, Chester Kinsman, they made a success of them both. We named the ranch, K2, for the father and son team that ran it. I've inherited everything . . . and just now, Casey, I have no great plans for expansion. I simply want to see our family holdings maintained and managed properly."

I thought that some day I'd like to have a thick mustache like Uncle Harry's. He smiled while he took a sip from his coffee cup. "When I heard that you were coming out west . . . well, I needed to make a decision that I'd been putting off. Vernon had been 'in training' with me so to speak. Instead of getting a good grasp of the family enterprise, he made a mighty mess of things. I had to ask him to leave, move out and get a job. I will continue to pay him a salary until he can find gainful employment."

He took a cigar from a box on the desk and continued. "You're several years younger than Vernon, yet not too young to begin learning the rudiments of business. I put no claim on you, Casey . . . nor do I make any promise to you. I certainly don't want another misfire down the road to deal with."

There was another pause while the cigar was lighted. "However, you are a bright lad with spirit. Learn as much as you're able this summer at K2. Ranching is interesting work and the men out there, as you've probably found already, are basically good folks to be around."

I saw a chance to jump in. "Uncle Harry, thanks for the opportunity. All I can say right now is that I'll give ranching my best shot."

"Good boy!" Uncle Harry leaned back and crossed his legs. "Casey, from the first, when I saw you walking back to me on the train platform and looking me square in the eye, I knew you had guts."

"Uncle Harry, my guts are feeling a bit queasy right now. Vernon has been out to K2. He's put pressure on me to get back on the train . . . leave town."

"Thunderation! I should have known he'd follow you out there! Do you think you can stick it out?"

"Yesterday I had my doubts, sir. But since I've learned to ride Jasper and made friends with Cal Paluskin, I've got a better chance of seeing it through."

"Cal Paluskin? Excellent! I couldn't have picked a better companion for you. And as for Jasper, if you like him, the horse is yours. No one else will ride him."

I was thrilled at this gesture. My own horse! Jasper is my very own horse! "Thank you, sir. I love Jasper!"

"Ride him all you want. Learn how far the ranch extends in all directions, Casey. That's enough of an assignment for you right now. Just learn what's going on at K2 and help out here and there, however your good judgment inclines you. You're a level-headed young man, but if there's trouble of any kind I want you to contact me immediately. There are no telephones out here, I'll show you a way to send a message before you leave tonight."

"I need your advice on something, sir."

"Sure. What is it?"

"I need to learn to swim."

Uncle Harry threw back his head and roared with laughter. Unaware that I'd almost drowned, his handsome face contorted in total merriment. "Casey, you're in exactly the right place for that!" Uncle Harry jumped out of his chair. "Come with me."

After striding through a number of hallways, we came to a large door in the very back of the manor. Uncle Harry quickly opened it and with a dramatic sweep of his arm, ushered me into an arena that contained a fair-sized indoor swimming pool.

"All three of my delightful daughters are like fish in this pond of ours. I'll arrange for Neva to pick you up twice a week for swimming lessons."

I was almost speechless. I ran over and dipped my hand into the cool, fresh water. I managed a thank-you and practically skipped back to the living room where Uncle Harry made the arrangements for my lessons.

The girls squealed with delight. Only Neva knew my serious purpose.

Colette chirped, "Leave it to us, Dad. We'll have him swimming like a salmon, quick as a wink." And she winked at me.

"B-but," I stammered. "I don't have a swim suit."

Colette, her pretty eyes twinkling, circled around me looking at my waist. Then she stuck her hand in my belt and tugged on it. "I can guess your size. I'd say a 24 inch waist. We'll get you a suit from town."

It was dusk. Time to go. On the way to the Ford, Uncle Harry told Sally to get something. Just before Neva and I pulled away, Sally came running out with a container covered with a cloth.

Uncle Harry handed the item to me. "If there's trouble, use this to contact me, Casey. Neva will tell how to use it." Uncle Harry helped Neva start the car and with a look of concern, he said. "Be careful out there."

I sat with the container on my lap for a few blocks. But when we got out into the country, I couldn't contain my curiosity any longer. I lifted the cloth cover and peered underneath. I was astonished to find a birdcage.

Neva chuckled, enjoying my puzzled expression. "It's a pigeon, Casey. Don't they have pigeons in New York?"

"Yes. Of course. When my mother and I visited Central Park, I used to take bread crumbs along to feed them. But how . . ." Then it came to me. This bird on my lap was a special kind of pigeon. I had Cal for a friend, Jasper to ride, and now my personal messenger. My stomach quit feeling queer; not quite so queasy anyway. Things were looking up.

eleven

A KNIFE IN MY TEETH

SUT FRITIPAN

The inside of my thighs ached; I wasn't used to a horse. My belly was sore from being kicked, but nothing would keep me awake tonight. Mostly it was a good sort of pain that came from tired muscles due to getting tight in the saddle . . . breaking in to a new life and making a place for myself. That felt good. With Uncle Harry's offer today, I was ready to lay it all on the line to make things work and learn about K2. I'd try to avoid trouble when I could, but confront it with everything I could muster if I had to.

When I'd handed the birdcage to Stella, she knowingly commented about pigeons.

"Every once in a while we use the little birds to send messages from here to Overton Manor, or from there out here." she explained. "We write the note on a little piece of paper, stick it in a small tube, then fasten it to the bird's leg."

She went on to say that, in my case, if I wanted to get help, I simply had to release the pigeon. Within half an hour, it would fly back to its roost at Overton Manor where Sally would probably see it and report its return to Mr. Kinsman. Before I headed to my room, I watched Stella place the pigeon in a wood and wire cage, called an aviary, where the K2 pigeons lived.

"I get it," I said. "Take one of these into town, release it, and it will fly back here."

Since Lobo wouldn't be coming in to guard me tonight, I took the precaution of bolting the sliding door. The windows were securely covered with latticework. Reassured, I snuggled down in the soft bed, with thoughts of riding Jasper up to Cal's hideaway in the morning.

I awoke to the crowing of a rooster. I finished another note to my mom just as Stella called me to breakfast.

"Cal came by last evening," said Stella as she placed a plate of ham and eggs in front of me. "He left a note and a nice piece of wild meat for you. I cooked the meat, sliced it up as part of your lunch."

"Ugh! Bear meat," I thought. Repelled by the idea of eating it, still, I decided that later on I'd give it a try.

"I assume that you'll be riding out again today?"

"Yes, Stella, thanks for putting up a lunch for me. I'll be back in time for dinner."

Cal's note included a map and directions to his hideaway. I was pleased to have this to take along; I still felt more at home on city streets than in the woods.

When I walked in to his stall, I was cheered by Jasper's whinny. I imagined him saying, "Good morning, friend Casey, are we going out riding again today?"

Chin Lee was in the barn and came over to watch me saddle Jasper.

"Looks like you got the hang of it," he observed. "But remember to cinch him up tight. Sometimes a horse will hold his breath and let it out after you think you've got it tight. Then when you mount up, the saddle can slide around."

I imagined the saddle sliding and dumping me off. "Wow, I sure wouldn't want something else for the hands to laugh at," I said.

As I gave him oats, Jasper bumped me with his nose and gave that little throaty sound I'd learned to love.

While we walked to the corral gate, I left word with Chin Lee where I would be going for the day. I didn't mention the hideaway, I simply said that Cal had offered to show me around some. As we approached the gate, I noticed a slim, older ranch hand standing a few feet from the gate.

"That's Sut. Sut Fritipan, over there," Chin Lee said. "He's an all-around hand. He's our cook when we're out on round-up, and probably our best rider too; a rodeo calf-roping champion to boot."

As I watched, Sut flipped his rope out and lassooed a fence post. He flipped the noose off and repeated the action.

I stopped to watch.

Sut must have seen me out of the corner of his eye. "Whata ya gawkin' at, Dude?"

"You've really got skill with that rope, Sut."

"Skill! What would a greenhorn know about anything!" Sut snorted. "Some just know how to fork down vittles they hain't earned and that don't take no skill at all."

Sut turned and glared at me.

"Everyone has to learn how to be useful." I answered.

"Well, while you're around here, Dude, just stay outa my way! I don't take kindly to wet-nosed city kids."

Chin Lee and I moved on. "Don't mind Sut a blowin' off," Chin Lee advised. "I think he's still sore and smartin' about having to put up with Vernon."

Sut had put me down hard. It helped my hurt feelings to know that Vernon had stirred up resentment that would naturally rebound against me as another Harry Kinsman nephew. It was with a sigh of relief that I mounted up. Sut's lashing out at me lingered on my mind. As Jasper and I headed for the hills,

I decided not to be thin-skinned about it. That lightened up my mood.

Within minutes I was following the map out past the far pasture, heading for Funnel Creek which wound its way down to empty into the Serpentine River.

I checked Cal's map and leaned down to Jasper's ear. "That looks like the trail-head up there." My fine companion whinnied a reply.

With a surge of joy, I followed the trail – along the brush growing by the stream, then up into timber country to a ridge along the north side of a ravine. The beautiful day made the slow going enjoyable. Jasper made the effort, I just relaxed in the saddle, gliding along with bright sun flashing through the treetops. I breathed deeply, filling my lungs with the cool, pine-scented air.

I found it hard to judge distance, but I guessed it to be a mile further on when the wooded area gave way to a small clearing. Near the center stood a lodge-pole pine and deerskin teepee. In front, a wisp of white smoke twirled up from a campfire. I gazed at Cal's rustic hideway , in every way a contrast to my New York City.

Just as I jumped off Jasper, Cal stepped out from behind a tree.

"Good. You got here before I have to leave. Come see Lobo's lean-to."

At the far edge of the clearing, Lobo lay on Cal's blanket in the shade of a shelter neatly made from pine boughs propped on a rectangle of poles, lashed together with rawhide.

Lobo wagged his tail a bit when I knelt beside him and gently stroked his tawny shoulder.

"He's better today, Cal observed. "He lapped up meat broth at sunrise. Soon you can give him more from that dish by the fire."

Cal asked, "Did Stella give you bear meat?"

"Yes. I'll have it for lunch."

"Uhunh. I have had two meals of it. We will be ready for trouble."

Trouble? Rapid-fire thoughts came to mind. I sensed that I'd better be ready . . . and not only to ward off the next attack. Cal knows we need to be strong. Yes, in mind and body . . . also smart, to see danger coming and react . . . but especially, I need to be savvy . . . quick to use what strengths we have to win.

Cal sat on a log by the fire opposite me. "Let the fire go out so the smoke won't attract attention. Stay back from Lobo. He needs to sleep."

I was embarrassed when Cal asked, "Did you check to see if you were followed up here? Danger will come on two feet."

"I didn't think of it."

"Uhunh. Next time, look back on trail, and then check like this . . . "

I was surprised to see Cal clear a small area of earth, lie down on his stomach, and drive the blade of a knife into the ground. Then, with his ear pressed to the earth, he clenched the knife's leather handle with his teeth. He covered his other ear with his hand.

He rose up after half a minute, wiping the six-inch blade on his thigh.

"No one on the trail near by." He sheathed the knife and handed it to me.

"Take this, I have another."

I took the knife from him. "Thank you. I am in your debt."

"I must get back to the ranch. Come down just before sunset. We will not meet on the trail. I will come back another way and spend the night on the ridge up there." He pointed up the hill.

Cal's horse was staked out in the woods. I heard it whinny as horse and rider moved away.

I took note of the fine steel of my new knife and fastened its sheath on the left side of my belt; quickly available to my right hand. Then I flattened out and tried Cal's listening method. Ear to the ground and teeth biting the knife, I thrilled to the sound of Cal's horse descending the trail.

Amazed at how far the horse's rhythmical hoof beats vibrated back to me, I lay motionless, savoring this bit of woodsy trail lore until the sound faded away. Then, at that very moment, I heard a faint thump, thump, thump. The muffled footsteps could be from a man stealthily climbing up the trail. As I listened, they became more distinct.

Noiselessly I rose and slipped behind a tall growth of fern where I cast my eyes down the trail. I recoiled at the sight of Vernon, rifle in hand, quickly moving to the edge of the hideaway clearing. A whip-like object dangled at his waist, and icy fear stabbed at my heart when I realized Vernon was stalking me! My first day at K2, while Vernon had watched, I'd been near death, almost drowning in the ditch. Now one false move would surely bring a bullet to my heart.

For a second I knew the blind terror of the rabbit that runs in circles at the sound of the baying hound. At first, frozen with fear, I sat with my head down, not even wanting to breathe . . . then clear thinking returned and I realized I had an advantage. Vernon didn't know I was up here. I could lie low, watching his every move. If he came close, I could spring on him with my knife.

Reassured, I watched with cool detachment as Vernon began to explore the camp with its teepee. My mind raced to Lobo and Jasper, both hidden from view in the thicket behind me. To find them, Vernon would need to come by me first.

Vernon peered in, poking his rifle into the teepee, but didn't enter it. He knelt by the fire pit and stirred the ashes. Next he stood tall and with a slow, penetrating stare, scanned the area. When his blazing eyes came to my clump of fern, my heart skipped several beats and a shiver ran up my spine. He suddenly shifted the gun to his other hand. But instead of shooting into my shield of greenery, he strode across the clearing and retreated back down the trail.

I used the knife again, listening to his retreating footsteps. I thanked God that Vernon hadn't seen Lobo. The big wolf-dog was still in safe hiding.

I sat dejectedly fighting off a depressed mood brought on by a cold reality of my life . . . Vernon wanted to kill me. Then I thought of Cal and my flagging spirits revived.

"Cal's a great companion to have during this time of trial," I said to myself. "I need him. Uncle Harry seems to be powerless to stop Vernon. It's true that I haven't told him how bad it's been for me, but what could my good uncle do to protect me anyway?"

As I walked to Lobo I had this thought, which made me go weak in the knees. I stopped, sat on a log, took off my hat and fanned my face.

There's so much at stake for the future of the Kinsman family holdings. This was still frontier territory. The question is, who will take over the reins of leadership from Harry Kinsman? There were strong women here, but in these times, only male leadership was accepted. My cousins would need someone like me to help maintain the family's position. There could be a mite of madness in Uncle Harry's method. Maybe he's standing back just to see if I'm smart enough and tough enough to pass this big test. If I survive Vernon's all-out war against me, then I would be fit to manage the Kinsman empire some day. And that would include even this beautiful forested place of natural beauty.

I stood up and looked down the wooded slope, out across the vast cattle range to the fields of grain and alfalfa in the distance. A strong puff of wind forced me to take a step back. It refreshed my face and stirred up my hair.

I lifted my heart: "Oh God, help me to know what to do, and give me the strength to do it."

Leaning into the fresh, chill wind, I felt a surge of courage. I shivered as a message came on the breeze . . . Confront the evil challenge and good will come from it.

Now I knew. I longed for that past time when Mom, Dad and I, with so few possessions, had known a happy, sheltered life in Brooklyn. But now my destiny was here . . . in the lush forest and green fields and with the caring Kinsman family I'd come to know and love.

I thought of the three cousins who were like loving sisters to me and made a vow to stick it out for them, for Aunt Louise, and yes, for Uncle Harry, too. I'm going to beat back Vernon's plan to drive me off. Then I'll bring Mom out here to live. And, some day, because I figure it's already his, maybe I can see to a deed for this hideaway with Calvin Paluskin's name on it.

twelve

SHOWDOWN AT SUNDOWN

VERNON

I breathed the woodsy air deeply and touched some sticky pitch oozing from a large fir tree on the way to check on Lobo. I noticed tamarack, the tree whose bright green needles would turn gold and then drop in the fall. I loved wildlife, as Cal did. On the forest floor he had pointed out wild strawberries, Oregon grape, fern and scrub oak.

Lobo gave a little whine when I knelt to stroke his big head and speak to him soothingly. He rose up enough to lap up the rest of the meat broth. Then it was time for my lunch. With an appetite sharpened from the forest's fresh air, I actually enjoyed the bear meat's wild flavor.

Afterwards, I thought: "Not bad. When trying out new food, it helps to be hungry."

The afternoon passed pleasantly. Jasper and I explored the far ridge and the area below. Once Jasper shivered and gave his throaty sound as a scream echoed through the forest.

"It's O.K., Jasper," I said, patting his neck. "I think that's just a cougar." Then I reassured myself by putting my hand to the knife at my belt. Full of bear meat, I didn't sense a problem with the big cat.

The routine for the next three days was much the same. Right after breakfast, Jasper and I would head up to the hideaway to relieve Cal. I'd spend each day talking to Lobo and exploring the hillside. Flies buzzed, bees flew in straight lines with a purpose, and once I came to a huge red ant-hill, easily three feet high.

Each day I'd discover new birds and small animals of the forest. Chipmunks, squirrels, and an occasional jack-rabbit scampered across the trail. But to my disappointment, I saw no ant-eaters, coyotes, badgers, or porcupines, though Cal had described them and told of their habits.

But then, as I wandered through a stand of tall pine, a small rabbit hopped onto the trail ahead and I looked up, startled to see a huge bird descending on it. Its powerful wings propelled it at lightning speed to pounce on its prey.

With talons embedded, the predator remained motionless as the rabbit's life-blood ebbed out onto the forest floor.

Though I was in no danger, a tingling shot up my spine as the large eyes of the fierce bird pierced me with its gaze. We stood transfixed in each others' unblinking stare for a hundred of my racing heartbeats. Then, still clutching the little animal, it spread its wings, shot into the air, and beat its way silently down the tree-lined corridor.

On the fourth day, the sun was low when Jasper and I trotted back into the clearing from a jaunt over to Funnel Creek. We found Cal tending Lobo with bear grease once again.

I described the kill of the day before.

"Uhunh. I saw the rabbit blood on the trail and this feather nearby."

Cal reached into his vest and produced a small gray feather. "It is from the goshawk. A pair of them have a nest near the crest, up from the creek. I hear their call every morning. They hatched four hungry young ones last month."

"Cal, I'm impressed by your awareness of what goes on in this part of the forest."

We parted company and I traveled the trail back to the ranch house. Neva came by just after I'd washed up and took me for my first swimming lesson.

Annie and Colette met us at the door and handed me a towel and a bright red swim-suit.

"Gee, thanks, gals," I shouted as I headed up to my room to change. I expected one or more of the cousins to get in with me and start my swimming instructions. But as I jumped in the cool water up to my waist, they sat on the edge of the pool in their cute one-piece suits.

Colette said, "We think this first time in the pool, you ought to be getting used to the water. Maybe you could put your hands on the side and kick." Then all three dove in and swam to the deep end.

I loved being in the pool and put my mind to this latest learning challenge. My ordeal in the irrigation ditch I put behind me. I even climbed up and jumped in several times, purposely sinking down before pushing off the bottom and shooting to the surface. The bubbles tickled my skin. What a thrill! I'd never before felt so pleasantly alive and carefree. My thighs and stomach muscles, still stiff and sore, limbered up in the soothing waters.

After about half an hour of this free activity Colette made another suggestion.

"Casey, you seem ready for pushing off from the edge."

She showed me how to hang on to the edge of the pool with my chin in the water, and, with steady kicking, push off a foot or two and paddle back with cupped hands. Colette called this the "dog paddle."

It worked! After a few minutes I no longer sank. Instead, I found myself moving back to the pool's edge, then I pushed away again and dog-paddled back. The success of this simple action gave me a thrill of pride. I was swimming!

After another pleasant dinner, Mrs. Boltus left the table and the rest of us gathered in the parlor. After Neva played a lively "Meet Me in St. Louis, Louie," on the piano, Aunt Louise handed the guitar to me. "Casey, would you play for us now?"

I was getting used to the guitar. I found the chords for "My Bonnie Lies Over the Ocean." I remembered the words for it and the others joined in the singing. Next I came up with "Clementine," and finished with one that we all seemed to especially enjoy: "Bye. Bye, Blackbird." Wow!

The windows were open and I'll bet they could hear us singing all the way down the street. I wondered what Mrs. Boltus thought of the family having so much fun together. Vernon would probably be enraged to hear that things were going so well at Overton Manor without him. If he knew, I was certain that he might try some desperate act against me. I would have to be very watchful.

Before my return to K2, I slipped into the library and, with a thrill of satisfaction, found a section in an encyclopedia on the goshawk. It read:

– a very powerful and aggressive bird of prey, measuring about 24 inches high, the largest of the hawk family. Found in Canada and some northern tier states, they feed mostly on birds, but also small animals. They hunt through thickets and woods, usually below the treetops.

Back at K2, I was getting ready for bed and almost jumped out of my skin when I heard a scratching sound at my sliding door. I whirled around and drew out my knife.

A voice came from outside. "We need a plan for tomorrow."

"Cal! I thought it might be Vernon out there."

He noted the knife. "Ununh. You know how to fight with a knife?"

"No. Come on in, Cal."

Cal came in and sat cross-legged on the floor. I described Vernon's visit to the hideaway.

"Ununh. I heard Sut talking to Vernon behind the barn. Vernon knows that you come up to the hideaway, but I don't think he knows why. They didn't talk of Lobo."

"Do they have a plan?"

"Vernon will follow your trail tomorrow. I go up now. Tonight I will build a dead-fall on the trail to catch him, you must be careful not to trigger it."

"A dead-fall, with a heavy object set to drop down, like on an animal?"

"Yes."

"Cal, Vernon is my bitter enemy, but I don't want to see him dead. Is there another way?"

"Ununh. There is another way. I'll go fix it. Get up early. Get to hideaway when the sun comes up . . . as soon as there is light to see the trail."

"I see. Vernon will think I'll be going up later, after breakfast. Earlier, I'll get up ahead him."

"We will lie in wait for him."

Cal handed me a pair of moccasins. "You should wear these on the trail."

I slipped out of my boots and tried them on. They were a perfect fit. "Again, Cal, I thank you. Sometime I'll find a way to repay you."

"Put moccasin toe down first, pointed in . . . like this . . . to move silent as a fox to its prey."

At the door, Cal turned. "Do you know the sound of the goshawk?"

I was startled to hear Cal give the bird-call, "Sreee sreee

sreee."

"Yes, I heard that call up near the hideaway ."

"The goshawk is larger, more powerful than his smaller brother, the hawk. The goshawk will repeat the cry many times. If you hear only three, you will know it is my signal for you to take cover quietly until danger passes."

I was amazed at this. Cal disappeared, and I followed him out and closed the door behind me. I slipped over to where the pigeon was kept. I knew that Vernon had a plan to make trouble for me tomorrow. I trusted Cal, but I'd promised Uncle Harry to contact him in case of danger. I found the aviary and opened the little wire door. In the gloom my eyes became accustomed to the dark and I saw the pigeon lying dead inside.

Awestruck at what must have been yet another move against my cutting off a call for help, I quickly returned to my room and to bed.

I fell asleep wondering. "When? When did the little bird die?" I guessed that Olga Boltus had seen me leave Overton Manor with the cage and had told Vernon. Somehow, he either killed the bird himself or had someone do it for him today. What a chilling thought.

I spent a restless night interspersed with wild dreams of crashing through under-brush, running from a pursuer I couldn't see. Finally I got up, ready to ride to the hideaway. I left Stella the usual note, found the rest of the bear meat she'd cooked for me, and tucked it in my knapsack, along with a chunk of bread and a large red apple.

Jasper murmured his usual throaty greeting as I saddled him. It was still quite dark as I led him through the paddock and the gate. I mounted up and we trotted toward the hills. A faint glow of the rising sun over my right shoulder gave sureness of true direction. I liked the shrill cry of a goshawk overhead and the scent of road-side grass, wet with dew. I tried to imitate the hawk's call. After several tries I began to get it right.

Unhurried, we jogged along in the sweet cool air of early dawn. I pulled out the apple and munched it for a quick breakfast on the trail. Ah! The life of the ranch hand! I knew full well my ranch life wasn't typical, but close enough for me to be attracted by this kind of living . . . close to animals, close to nature, basic relationships with others. God in heaven, I loved it! I felt a little foolish, when "Home on the Range" came to mind and I sang out:

"Oh give me a hooome . . . Where the buffalo roooam . . . Where the deer and the antelope plaaay."

Jasper liked my singing, he whinnied and seemed to join in by tossing his head up and down.

"Where seldom is heard . . . a discouraging word . . . and the skies are not cloudy all daaaaay."

I came to the trailhead just as the dawning sun's gold- and salmon- colored rays spread across the ridge. I reined up and scanned the spot where Cal said he would spend the night. He could be watching me from up there. I looked back on the trail. Sure that no one followed, I didn't use the knife to check further.

It was full daylight when I entered the clearing of the hideaway. This morning, Lobo not only sprang up from his bed, he quickly came over to me and with the big animal's greeting came a surge of pure joy. We'd saved this good old dog. I also noted that Cal had fastened Lobo with a leash and collar, both from braided rawhide, to prevent his return to K2 before he was well enough.

Two pots stood by the fire. One contained bear meat swimming in broth, the other had a stirring stick stuck in a strange smelling stew of some kind.

Cal appeared and sat cross-legged on the ground.

"Lobo is much better today." I began.

"Ununh. He is eating meat and will soon run."

I lifted the stick from the sticky mixture and wrinkled my nose. Is this for Lobo?

"No. I mix pitch, gum, and wild honey, over the fire . . . not for the dog, not for us. Look over your shoulder down the hill half way. See the honey tree with bees swarming around it."

"Yes."

"Good for you to stay away from it. That's where I shot the bear."

Realizing Cal's reluctance to say more, I didn't ask further about the strange concoction.

"Will Vernon come up here today?"

"He said he would. I talked to Bernie; asked for the day off."

Cal continued. "Tether Jasper at the far side over by my horse. It's best if you stay in camp all day."

I nodded agreement. I didn't mind. I was anxious about Vernon, but while we waited for him to make his move, I'd just tend to Lobo and observe the fine points of nature in and around the clearing.

Cal went on. "I will be up on the ridge. If I see anyone at the trailhead, I'll signal with the goshawk call. If you hear it, take cover where you can see anyone on the trail, but they won't see you."

The day passed slowly but pleasantly. Cal had eaten some of the meat from the pot before he left and I ate a bite of it before feeding the rest of it to Lobo at mid day.

"If there's anything to Cal's belief that the bear's strength can be given to us through this meat," I thought as I ate my lunch, "all three of us should be ready to take on the Cardiff Giant."

I hadn't thought of books and reading lately. When the myth of the giant popped into my head, I began to think of other stories and felt a pang of longing. I missed reading. The next time I went in for swimming, I'd ask about the Overton Manor library.

I was drowsy after lunch. Lobo was sleeping and I had to fight to keep awake. I forced myself to think of a story I'd read from <u>The Jungle Book</u>. Rudyard Kipling's character, Mowgli, a boy of India, came to mind. One adventure that involved a huge snake called a boa constrictor, put me in mind of mysterious monkeys, tigers and snakes.

Snakes. I wondered idly why I hadn't seen any snakes around here. I thought, fancifully, that maybe K2 was like Ireland where, I'd heard, St. Patrick had dispelled the snakes into the sea.

I must have dozed off, because the figure of a fierce pirate appeared with a big bird on his shoulder. The bird cried out, "Sree, Sree, Sree!" And the pirate raised his sword and charged.

I shook myself awake, tense, but greatly relieved to be free of the bad dream. Lobo still rested quietly. I began to relax again. How long had I napped? The sun, low and about to set, prompted the thought: "Has Cal tried signal me?"

Several minutes passed and long shadows were cast across the clearing when I got up, fully alert. Then I shivered at a goshawk's cry . . . that stopped short at three. I remembered Cal's words, "the real goshawk will repeat the cry many times." I'd received the warning and it came from just up the ravine. Cal was on his way down!

I silently crossed to the thicket and awaited developments. Vernon would probably tether his horse below so he could sneak up here looking for me on foot.

From the thicket, I had a clear view of the last fifty yards leading up to the hideaway. Wide awake with excitement, I could feel my heart pounding.

Then, in the sun's fading rays, it happened! The silhouette

of a man came into view. Moving cautiously, the figure came closer.

Then I started up, shocked to see another figure silently and swiftly attack the man on the trail and disappear. A piercing scream of agony froze my blood and sucked the breath from me. The man on the trail thrashed his way back down the mountain with one long, drawn-out wail after another.

I quickly ran to the spot of the attack. There, in the dim light, lay Cal's pot, empty of the strange pitch and honey mixture, but crawling with large red ants. Another ugly thing lay in the dust. I picked it up. It was a weapon as long as my arm made of tightly woven leather, with a whip handle on one end and a leather bag on the other. I could feel lead pellets laced inside. This could be the instrument that had almost killed Lobo!

I rushed back to find Cal leading both horses into the clearing. I didn't let him see the whip-like weapon as I slipped it into my saddlebag.

Before I had a chance to speak, Cal said, "Lobo will be all right by himself tonight. You and I must get back to K2. Follow me, we'll go a different way."

Without hesitation, I mounted up and galloped down the hill behind Cal and his horse. My recent riding experience allowed me to keep up with Cal's swift descent by slacking the reins, giving Jasper his head. In much less time than it took to return the other way, we soon loped along with the ranch house in sight. Then Cal pulled up and waved me on by. I understood that it would be best if we weren't seen riding in together.

At dinner with Bernie and Stella, I talked about riding out and getting to know more about K2. I assumed no one was the wiser. The next day, I found a hiding place for Vernon's whip between two boards in the barn.

thirteen

SUT LASSOES TROUBLE

Day after day passed by without incident. I knew it must have been Vernon who'd had the "mixture" dumped on his back up there on the trail, but no one at K2 said anything about it. Another day dawned and I waited impatiently for Neva to pick me up for a swimming lesson and dinner.

Lobo continued to improve, so Cal cut me loose from the need to spend time at the hideaway. Instead, I busied myself with other things, spending hours in the barn. There were two cows at K2. It had been Lobo's job to get them from the pasture each afternoon. Now I rode out and brought them in, and Chin Lee taught me how to milk them. I learned about chickens . . . cleaning the hen house, then spreading the manure around under the apple and cherry trees. I liked putting fresh straw under the roosts. I liked picking eggs from the nests each morning.

I rode out with Bernie; watched him change irrigation water from one field to another, and helped him replace fence posts when needed. I liked the work, though a ranch hand got paid very little beyond room and board. The thought came to me every night as I drifted off to sleep, "I'm learning to be a ranch hand." Next, I might try my hand with a lasso.

Early the next week Neva came driving the buckboard in just after lunch and waited while I got ready for the ride into town. On the way in, I told her about the dead pigeon.

Neva reacted with shock. "Casey! I'm just sure that whoever killed the pigeon didn't want you to contact Dad for help!"

"Yes, and meant it as a warning as well."

"Just be careful, Casey," Neva said, with a worried look.

I quickly changed the subject with a request for her to teach me how to drive the horse-drawn wagon. I picked it up quickly and was pleased to have the reins as we wound our way down the driveway to the back of the house.

After another swimming lesson, where I practiced the stroke called the crawl, we changed out of suits and met again for dinner.

I really enjoyed the dinners and looked forward to them. As mouth-watering odors came from the kitchen, I took my place at the table.

There had been the tumult of one perilous challenge after another, but since the incident on the hill, Vernon hadn't created any new problem for me. But now, just before Uncle Harry began the usual thanks for the meal, Vernon walked in and quietly took a seat at the table across from me. He greeted everyone pleasantly and then looked at me.

After we gave thanks for the meal, he said mildly, "It's time we met, Casey. I'm Vernon Boltus. My mother, Olga, has told me some about you . . . from the east I hear. It must be quite a change for you. I understand you lived in a tenement house."

I wanted to shout, "You hypocrite, pretending we've not met!" But I was too shocked to respond.

Vernon had changed his look of hatred to a sweet smile as

he helped himself to the mashed potatoes. "And I hear from the farm hands that you have taken to ranch life. As a greenhorn I hope you haven't blundered into trouble. You've been cleaning out stalls and hen-houses . . . good activity for you, I would think. Spreading manure is much less hazardous for you than aimlessly wandering around irrigation ditches."

I desperately strove to deflect Vernon's latest form of attack. This cleverly worded verbal abuse was like fending off a swordsman out of <u>The Three Musketeers</u>. I struggled to think of a reply.

Vernon went on with an infuriating smirk. "Then too, one can be useful bringing the in cows from pasture. But ordinarily that's a job for a dog, is it not?"

Lobo! Shock gave way to seething anger at the mention of the big dog. Clearly Vernon in a war of words had the nerve to sit there gloating, taunting me about the beautiful animal he tried to brutally beat to death!

I replied with a coolness that masked my true feelings.

"Actually, Vernon, I have had some adventures at K2, but I think even the lowest chore can be educational." I paused to meet his steely stare with a smile.

"I also hope to find railroading interesting. I understand that even a simple action, such as billing out a boxcar of potatoes to its proper destination, can be challenging at times."

At this reference to his blunder, Vernon turned red with rage and his expression of hatred returned for all to see. By contrast, Neva gave me a wide-eyed look of admiration.

Uncle Harry broke in with a loud, "Uh hum!" He leaned forward, "Yes, Casey, Vernon makes a point and you seem to support it. What can I say? Young people need to grasp the importance of the basic jobs as part of the larger operation, be it ranching or railroading ."

This mild statement ended the verbal jousting. Mrs.

Boltus asked Vernon to tell us of a job offer, and he went on to boast of an interview with the manager of the local farm implement and feed store. Then Colette gave us a chuckle as she described the antics of her cat, and later on, with Aunt Louise's encouragement, I told of my pleasant music sessions with Mr. Lambrusco.

During the usual after-dinner piano and guitar concert, Neva and I played a few songs and everyone, including Vernon and his mother joined in the singing. I finished with "Bye Bye Blackbird." It would have been my fondest wish to forever bid goodbye to the black-hearted Vernon.

When the little concert ended and the family left the room, Vernon came up behind me as I reached up to place the guitar on the piano. He gave me a painful jab in the ribs with his elbow. "Get out or die!" he hissed. As he quickly moved away I saw a bald patch on his upper neck. It looked raw with bright red spots. Could the irritation have been caused by a woodsy potion spiced with red ants?

On the way back, Neva eagerly spoke of the dinner conversation.

"Casey, Vernon baited you terribly, but you really hit him hard with his potato shipment goof. Dad must have been impressed by the way you faced Vernon down."

"Well," I replied, "thanks to you, I knew about the miss-sent car of spuds."

Neva went on. "Dad thinks it's time you rode Jasper in to Overton Manor. Not that I mind coming for you, actually I'll miss our rides together. But now that you're riding so well, you can be independent."

"That strikes me as a good idea, Neva," I responded, glad to change the subject. "Even though I'll miss our rides too."

"Mom has invited you for dinner the day after tomorrow. We'll expect you about 3:30 for swimming."

I prepared for bed with a heavy heart. As I reflected on the Overton visit, the dinner had gone well, but my sore ribs reminded me of Vernon's latest attack. The pain in my side kept me awake most of the night.

Just after sunrise and groggy from lack of sleep, I shuffled in to shower, standing in the cool stream until my head cleared. I prayed for a good day and forced down a quick breakfast before jogging out to help Chin Lee repair a broken pump in the cabin where the Tyson family lived. Mr. Tyson, the K2 blacksmith, needed my help at the forge. I pumped the bellows for the glowing charcoal fire, as he fashioned a new swivel for his pump handle. Back in the kitchen I got to know Mrs. Tyson while Chin Lee and I made the repair at the sink.

Mrs. Tyson spoke of her five children. "They've taken to you, Casey," she began. "There are no other children around for them to play with. Naturally they're drawn to any younger person who visits here."

When we finished our repair, Mrs. Tyson smiled her appreciation.

"Sure glad to have the pump working again. The girls have been hauling water from the main house." She stopped stirring a pot on the stove to look at me. "Billy's our oldest at twelve, an' growin' up fast. Casey, would you maybe spare a minute to visit with him some?"

Billy, one of two boys, seemed old for his age. I found him sitting on his dad's saddle in the shed out back of the cabin. Still feeling listless, I watched Billy practicing with his lariat.

He noted my interest. "Look, Casey." He paused to pay out a loop. "This part is easy. It's twirling the loop around over your head and giving it just the right forward toss, that's kinda tricky."

I watched and asked questions as, time after time, Billy made a loop, vigorously gave two twirls of the rope, and then lassoed a stepladder.

Hoping to encourage him, I said, "Billy, you're going to be a true cowboy before you know it."

"You betcha boots I am!" Came the quick reply. "I'll soon be out there tendin' cattle. And if," he continued, "there's a calf that needs ropin' I'll drop a loop over its head, and tie t'other end on the saddle. A good cow-pony will take up the slack, so's I can jump off and truss the little critter up."

Billy looked at me and frowned. "Gotta be careful though. My dad says when gettin' on and off a horse you always hafta be sure not to get your boot caught in the stirrup. If that happens and you fall, the horse don't know any better and will drag you. Dad had a friend that got hisself killed just that very way."

Billy let me try my hand at tossing the loop at the ladder. After several clumsy attempts I finally got one to drop. Overall, the pleasant visit with the Tysons had brightened my dark mood.

At lunch, Bernie asked me to ride to the post office for him. On the return trip, heavy clouds spread overhead.

I spurred Jasper to move a little faster. "Looks like it might rain, boy."

A breeze sprang up. I squinted up at the cloud only to see a loop of rope sailing though the air. It dropped over my head and arms. I'd been lassoed like a yearling calf!

I could imagine being pulled off and dragged. An instant before my attacker jerked the rope taut, I grabbed the rope in front, leaned forward and looped it over my pommel. The rope encircling me snapped tight, biting into my arms. But because the loop included the pommel, I wasn't pulled off. Instead, I heard a grunt of surprise and I looked around to see Sut, the champion roper, careen from his horse. He'd been holding his rope with both hands. Startled when my end of the rope held fast to my saddle, he'd been jerked forward. Unable to regain his balance as his horse instinctively moved back, Sut had toppled into the dust. With his rider down, Sut's horse ran ahead, which allowed me to loosen the loop around me and cast it off. But Sut's rope still hung on my pommel.

Sut's horse slowed enough for me to catch up and grab his reins. I spoke soothingly, "Easy now, fella, easy there."

I spurred Jasper to a trot and thrilled to the feel of Sut's horse responding to a gentle pull on his reins. "Talk about turning the tables on Sut," I thought, as I coiled up Sut's rope, "now I have both his rope and his horse."

Lightning flashed across the sky. Sut's shouted obscenities mixed with a peal of thunder. I ignored the screaming as Sut ran, trying to catch us. It began to rain as Jasper and I, leading Sut's horse, trotted toward K2. I thought ahead, imagining surprised ranch hands looking up in amazement as I rode in, leading Sut's horse. But I decided to avoid that scene.

My close call left me light-headed. I could imagine how my being roped might have gone. After dragging me to death, Sut could have stuck my boot in one of Jason's stirrups to fake evidence of an accidental death of an inexperienced rider.

My heart still pounded as I pondered the next move. What had prompted Sut's attack? I suspected Vernon had put him up to it. Should I ride in and file a complaint with the sheriff? What would I say? Sut could claim that I had stolen his horse. With no witness to back me up, I'd have no way to refute that version of what had happened. No! I had to think of another way.

I turned around and headed back. In the distance, Sut was trudging along in the rain. When we met on the trail, I circled Sut at a safe distance with the horses heeding my guiding hand.

"Sut!" I called out. "Before I return your horse to you, we need to get something straight.

"First, I'm not going to blame you for what happened back there. I know someone put you up to it."

Sut stopped and stared in silence.

"I don't want to stir up more trouble than I already have. In fact, I could use some help to survive out here. I need you to help me."

I waited a few seconds. "How about it? Can I count on you?"

Sut remained silent.

"Here's your horse," I shouted as I dropped the reins. "Later on, give me an answer yes or no about helping . . . then, either way, you'll get your rope back too."

I left Sut moving to his horse as Jasper and I galloped back to the K2 barn. He'd want his rope back, so I'd get a chance to talk with him. I prayed that Sut would come around. Before I called it a day, I deposited the prize-winning rope in the barn wall where I'd hidden Vernon's leather weapon.

fourteen

JUGGLING ATTITUDES

After breakfast I decided to take the morning off from ranch work. I got the urge to join the Tyson children who were playing kick-the-can on the lawn. I remembered that I'd brought a bag of five juggler's balls from New York, and pulled them out of my grip with the Tyson children in mind.

Billy and two of his sisters welcomed me to their game. After several minutes, we sat resting in the shade and Billy asked, "What's in the bag, Casey?"

I got surprised looks as five red rubber balls rolled out.

One of the girls exclaimed, "Oh! What do you do with them?"

"I juggle them."

They squealed sounds of excitement.

I picked up a ball in each hand. "A kindly old man in New York taught me how to do this."

I showed them the two-ball rotating motion. The Tyson children sat silently watching my every move. When I swept up another ball and juggled with three, Billy exclaimed, "Wow."

All eyes got big as I snatched up a fourth ball, smoothly keeping all in the air.

I enjoyed the success of the little show. I needed this playful time to get my mind off my troubles.

I sang: "Oh! I come from Alabama with a banjo on my knee.

Goin' to Louisiana, my true love for to seeee."

I expanded my act by tossing one ball high while keeping the others moving. I put my hand under my knee, caught the high one on its way down and effortlessly continued on as before.

Without dropping a ball once, I sang two verses of "Camptown Racetrack."

I added variations, once catching a ball behind my back, then way out front. I began to draw a crowd. Four ranch hands came over. Then, out of the corner of my eye, I saw Stella and Mrs. Tyson who held her small daughter. As the baby watched, she giggled and laughed. I caught a glimpse of Sut Fritipan too.

I heard a gasp of appreciation as I knelt down, still juggling, and picked up the fifth ball, tossing it high in the air before bringing it into play with the rest.

As I juggled, I rattled off a spiel.

"The vaudeville juggler, on a bad night, dropped several balls and gets booed by the audience. After the show, the manager comes up and says, 'there's one big difference between you and the guy with the dog act.'"

"'What's that?' asks the juggler.

"'The man with the dog act is gonna get paid.'"

I got a few smiles so I made up a corny joke.

"The ranch hand asked his friend for help. He says, 'I'd like to ask your sister, Sheena, to the barn dance, but I'm shy with girls.'

"The friend told him to go up to his sister and say, 'Sheena, I thought, for a change, you might like to get out of the house.

Why not go with me to the barn dance.'

"So the shy hand practiced his spiel, knocked on her front door and stammered, 'Sh-Sheena, I – I thought you might like to get out of the barn for a change. Why not dance with me to the out-house?'"

This brought on hilarious laughter. The folks liked my little juggling act. The pretty red balls caught the bright morning light, flying up and down non-stop. I enjoyed running through my routine.

Near the end, I called out, "get set to catch a ball!"

In rapid succession I flipped each ball out as, one at a time, they dropped to my right hand.

I threw the first to Billy, the next to Stella, who almost dropped it. The third and fourth balls I lobbed to Chin Lee and Cal. The last one I zipped to Sut in back. He caught it easily and then stood there with a look of approval.

I went around collecting the balls. When Sut handed over his, he quietly asked, "Meet me behind the barn?" His pleasant tone of voice seemed friendly enough.

"When?"

"Five minutes?"

I nodded. "Five minutes it is."

My happy little show over, the dark cloud of Vernon's hatred returned. I said a short prayer that Sut would help me, or at least, no longer be a threat.

Those who had seen my act liked it. Chin Lee gave me a pat on the back. Stella came over with her little girl.

"Well, young man," she began happily, "I don't recollect we've seen anything like that before. Right entertaining it was. Hope you'll give another show when Bernie and Mr. Tyson can see it."

I told her I could, then promised Billy I'd give him juggling lessons in exchange for rope lessons.

Walking slowly, so as not to attract attention, I moved to the barn, eager to meet with Sut. On the way I noticed a pigeon fly down and land in its aviary. I thought: "That's why they call them 'homing pigeons.' That one lived here, and had flown back home." Vernon might have taken this one with him back to town when he'd killed the other one.

fifteen

THE BREAKING POINT

I put the red balls away, except for one that I idly tossed while waiting for Sut.

Sut called to me from a barn window. "Hey, there, Mr. Showman," he began. "When do I get my rope back?"

"You'll get it back soon enough. First, how about some answers."

"Well, Young Fella, I had you figured wrong at first. You got a lotta sand to stick it out here. I won't try anything else to discourage you."

"How about out there when you dropped the loop over me. Were you going to drag me?"

"Naw! I couldn't do that. I'm a rodeo man. I wouldn't do that to nobody!" Sut leaned over the window sill. "I was jus' fixin' to scare you into headin' back where you came from."

"Did Vernon put you up to it?"

"Yeah, but I don't owe him a thing."

"Is he sending messages to you by pigeon?"

Sut looked startled. "How'd you know that?"

"Someone killed the pigeon I brought out here. Messages by pigeon had to figure into the plot against me."

Sut straightened up. "You've got most of it figured out. Give me back my rope and I'll tell you the rest of what I know."

While Sut waited at the window, I circled around, and entered the barn. I got the rope and walked up to him with it in my hand. "Here, now what do I need to know?"

"Vernon rode in the same night you got back, and musta killed your pigeon. He rousted me outa my bunk and said that you were gonna be bad for K2." Sut smiled and scratched his chin. "After seeing you on Jasper the first time, it wasn't hard for me to believe you'd make a mess of things out here."

"Yeah, and how do you feel about that now?" I asked as I handed over the rope.

"You learned ridin' fast and handled yourself like a drover when you and I had our little go 'round last night." Sut reached over and took his rope. "I'm on your side now."

I looked Sut hard in the eye. "Thanks, what else?"

"Vernon's hell-bent to get you; probably on his way out here right now. He might send me a message."

"A pigeon flew in just now," I said with a question in my eyes.

With a "wait here," Sut slipped smoothly through the window. In two minutes he was back with a little message tube in his hand. "Here," Sut said. "You read it."

The message read:

Today at noon.
Casey at trailhead
or Neva will suffer.

Or Neva will suffer? That did it! All those foul things done to me mattered little compared to threatening Neva! Now I punched the air in a seething fury.

Sut shook his head. "This is bad. What you want me to

do?"

"Help me saddle up!"

We rushed to the barn and Jasper, with his whinny, seemed to sense the excitement.

I fought to remain calm. "Thanks for your offer to help, Sut, but it's up to me to put a stop to Vernon's threats. He's on the mountain . . . waiting for me . . . got to give it my best shot."

Seconds later I rode out. Dreading the thought of Vernon lying in wait, I was spurred on by repeating . . . "give it your best shot." He may be too much for me, but I have a chance to end this . . . stop him from wrecking our lives.

sixteen

AMBUSH AT NOON

I spurred Jasper to a gallop. At the trailhead, I jumped off, wary of an ambush, and shouted, "Vernon! Come on! Let's get it over with!" Silently I prayed for help.

Vernon had to be stopped. I picked up a stick to keep my hand from shaking. If I simply got on the train to Seattle, Vernon would still be a menace. If anything, my leaving town would worsen Vernon's relationship with Uncle Harry. Now Neva had been threatened!

Vernon's horse might be nearby. I held my breath and listened. At first there was only a faint rustle of leaves. Then, from up on the hill, came a sound like a horse's whinny.

I moved toward the sound. Up ahead Vernon had suffered with Cal's awful mixture of pitch and ants on his neck. Maybe something even more terrible would lie in wait for me.

A steady walk up the trail showed nothing unusual. I drew my knife, terrified at the thought of having to fight Vernon hand to hand.

Then, my foot caught a tripwire cleverly set to trigger a rock-slide. Frantically I dove forward. Big rocks bounced by, and one bashed my thigh.

Screaming with pain, I rolled over clutching my leg, hoping and praying I'd still be able to walk. The boulder had broken the skin, but had not snapped the bone. Blood seeped through my pants, but as the shock wore off, I managed to scramble to my feet and stagger on, still clutching my knife. Relieved that I'd survived the first attack, I tried to ignore the pain and devise a plan. Limping up to where the rock-slide had been set, I searched for tracks.

I saw a cord attached to a small log. The cord ran down the hill and across the trail to the point where I'd kicked it. The log had held back a pile of rocks that had been collected from the hillside. I'd walked into a clever trap. Boot tracks on the hillside led to the place where the rocks had been stacked. From there, the boot tracks led to a clearing where they mixed with hoof-prints that led up the hill.

I surveyed the surrounding area. Vernon no doubt waited up ahead. What would he spring on me next?

I told myself, "Think like him. What would I do if I were in his boots?"

I hadn't heard hoof beats. My blood enemy had ridden off before I had triggered the slide. Hiding near enough to hear my scream, he would not go on until he was sure that I'd survived and had seen me pick up his trail. If so, he'd be watching me right now!

I whipped around and caught sight of him, as a man's head ducked back into dense shrubbery on the ridge above.

I drove my knife into the ground, fell beside it, and clamped my teeth on its handle. I counted the seconds as I heard my attacker move on. I knew from the horse's gait that a man was leading it. I counted to sixty-four before they stopped. So! A minute's walk beyond the ridge I could assume Vernon would spring his next move!

I waited another half minute to be sure, but heard only the

shuffle of a tethered horse.

The many hours spent in these woods during Lobo's healing time came in handy now. I knew the silent way to move on the trail, and when I'd gone out to play with the Tyson children this morning, I'd worn the deer-skin moccasins that Cal had given me. Now I could move swiftly and silently to the next encounter.

Despite the pain in my leg, I moved along, counting the seconds. Moving parallel to the ridge, I intended to get past his place of ambush before I moved up and over. I counted sixty-four seconds, cut left, and stealthily approached the point up where, according to my calculation, Vernon had stopped. Yes! I could see his horse in a small clearing!

My thigh throbbed so painfully I had to move. Cautiously, I drew closer, moving low to the ground, making each step noiselessly. Skirting Vernon's horse, I hid behind a growth of scrub oak. The pain prompted me to move again, but just then, Vernon quickly came out of a thicket, mounted his horse and slowly rode down the hill. He was following a rough animal trail that probably led to the river's edge a few hundred yards away.

This was the time and place for a showdown. But until Vernon stopped and dismounted again, I had no chance.

Blood trickled down my leg. I knew a basic instinct of survival, inflamed by pain, an inner voice that screamed for caution . . . common sense urged me to turn back. But I doggedly plodded along at a safe distance behind the horse and rider . . . impelled by my love for the family who had been threatened by the fiendish young man ahead. As minute after minute went by, I was unable to devise a plan of action.

On and on I stumbled down the hill for what I judged to be an hour before Vernon pulled up. I watched him dismount, tie the horse to a tree limb and walk off into the woods. I heaved a sigh of relief and sank down behind a small fir. The evergreen smell of it reminded me of Christmas. Light-headed and weary from the loss of blood, I began to day-dream. A sob welled up at the thought of the upcoming holidays at Overton Manor. Would I be there to share the warmth of family love this Christmas?

Then I fought down the despairing thought as my primal instincts of survival resurfaced. I had let down my guard. I shook off the distraction . . . but too late! Vernon had sneaked up on me from behind. I turned in panic only to see him swinging a heavy club at my head.

I awoke engulfed with pain from the blow on my head and the stinging torture from hundreds of sharp needle-like stabs on my face, neck, and arms. In total panic I rolled and fell screaming from a mound to the forest floor. Writhing in a nightmarish frenzy, I realized that Vernon, who now stood watching me with gleeful enjoyment, had draped me over a huge ant-hill. I was covered with the crawling, biting, little red devils. In sheer panic I felt their sharp bites moving up my pant legs.

My caution on the trail had availed me nothing. Vernon had used his horse as a distraction. As I frantically fought off the ants, a rope pinned my arms to my sides. With a fiendish cry of victory, Vernon danced up and threw another loop around me and then another. Leaping to his horse, he spurred it to a gallop. The rope snapped tight as I was jerked off my feet, and began to bump and slide down the trail.

I screamed, "No! Nooo!" The worst had happened! Nothing is more terrifying than being dragged over bumps, rocks and limbs at high speed.

seventeen

THE LAST EFFORT

Bouncing over the trail at end of Vernon's rope, I suffered excruciating pain. Suffocating dirt filled my mouth and nose while face, arms and legs were lacerated. I knew I would die from injuries and the horrible torture of it. A terrifying thought flashed through my mind. If the dragging stopped while I was still conscious, then I'd die a slow, agonizing death. Oh! How horrible! And at that very moment the horse did stop and I writhed in total misery, choking out, "My God! Don't let me die like this!" How long would I lie here rolling around in agony before death came to release me? Hours . . . maybe days.

My enemy jumped off his horse, shouting, insanely, "At last! I've got you where I want you!"

I dimly heard the sound of rushing water. I'd been dragged to the Serpentine's muddy bank. Vernon quickly pulled his rope loose and gloated over my bleeding body shouting, "Wanna sing me a song, City Boy?" Vernon laughed hysterically: "Ha ha ha. How about 'Bye Bye Blackbird?' Ha ha ha."

He shrieked, "Bye bye, City Boy. Good riddance!" and kicked me, again and again . . . down the slippery riverbank.

But then, as Vernon was poised to give me the final kick, there came a loud bark and from out of the woods bounded Lobo. With a fierce snarl, the wolf-dog shot through the air at the one who had almost beaten him to death. Vernon turned as the animal sprang upon him and I heard his agonizing scream of desperation while man and beast splashed into the stream.

I'd saved Vernon once from Cal's plan to trap him in a deadfall, but I couldn't save him now. Still, I cried out, "Lobo!"

My tortured scream sounded more hawk-like than human as I helplessly slid down the muddy embankment into the river's swirling current.

At first, the water inflamed my pain. Every ant bite, cut and bruise radiated massive misery beyond my ability to bear it. My submerged gurgling shriek of anguish went nowhere.

Then the stinging eased as the soothing, ice-cold waters numbed my wounds and my will to live ebbed back.

With lungs about to burst, I felt a push from behind as I broke through to the surface. A fit of coughing cleared the dirt from my nose and throat, and I breathed in deep gasps of pure air. It came to me that once again Lobo had saved me from drowning, and now Colette's swimming lessons played a vital part. Struggling in the surging Serpentine, I came to where Funnel Creek flowed in. Helplessly caught in the confluence of the two streams, I barely stayed above the waves, sputtering . . . gasping.

With the icy waters came a sharper awareness of my wounds. I had no sight in my throbbing left eye. Open wounds on my thigh, buttocks and left shoulder left a crimson trail in the water.

Lobo swam past me to shore as I did a side-stroke to the river bank and lay on my back in the soothing mud. My shirt a rag, and pants ripped almost off, the mid-day sun glared down and fired up my unprotected wounds. I raised up in search of shelter, but saw only short grass and weeds. I lifted my hand to my head and discovered a massive bump, an eye swollen shut, and a bloody mass at my nose. The taste of blood convulsed my stomach. At least the ants were gone.

Attracted by blood, a swarm of stinging flies gathered around and settled in. I began to despair as I heard the echo of my primal screams. Miles from help I would die miserably . . . unless . . . unless I rolled myself back into the water while I still had the strength to do so. It would be easy . . . sinking into the cool, deep, water . . . relaxing. Death would be merciful.

"But no!" said my spirit, "that would be wrong."

Instead, I grasped a nearby shrub, and snapped off a stem with some leaves attached. With my good right arm, I used it to fan the flies away.

I worried about Vernon. If Lobo had left him to help me, maybe my enemy could still come back and finish me off. And I thought, "What's happened to Lobo? Had the intelligent animal gone for help?"

Minutes, then maybe an hour passed. I slipped in and out of a hellish delirium where I tumbled down a dusty hillside covered with rocks and brush . . . then the stinging flies roused me and the horror of my living nightmare returned in full.

Once, as blackness swept in, I prayed, "God in Heaven let this be it! Take me, take my pain!"

Then I became fully conscious, but thank God, not to the same miserable state. Instead, I sensed miraculous solace from head to toe. Had I crossed into the next world? No. But I felt surprise at the coolness of a damp cloth cleansing my wounds, and sure hands applying something medicinal.

I slipped back into blackness with the thought, "It's Cal. He salved Lobo's wounds and saved him." My heart swelled with love and gratitude. "Cal will save me too."

The sun, low to the hills, no longer seared my skin. Instead, I became aware of caring hands lifting me into the fold of a blanket. Seconds later, I dimly sensed movement and a scraping sound at my feet. As we gently moved back on the trail, I looked up to sun-tinged clouds and likened them to the celestial abode of angels, and Cal's travois seemed a sweet chariot carrying me home. Unlike Casey, the engineer, I had survived my violent encounter.

What simple happiness! A light breeze carried a mixture of cool, musty scents from the woods that stimulated my delighted spirit. My soul soared to the heights and spread to the breadth of my being. So close . . . so near to death . . . now supremely at one with the majesty of creation around me. Overhead, the sun sparkled through the bright green canopy of spruce and pine as I traversed this same stretch of woods for the second time today . . . each time pulled by a horse. I smiled at the irony of that . . . and yes, I much preferred this return trip.

I fought to remain conscious . . . just to savor the sweet sensation of life. Yet, when we came to the main trail, sleep of sorts swallowed me up and I ascended to perfect peace.

eighteen

THE WAY BACK

As I walked out to the Ford with Neva holding one arm and Uncle Harry the other, I heard Neva say cheerfully, "Well, Casey, only one week in the hospital and now you're back on your feet again."

Most of the time I must have been out of it. The nurses told me that when the delirium returned, they'd held me down, as I screamed, "No! Nooo! Don't leave me here to die!" Now, even with a patch over my left eye, and showing scars on my nose and face, I'm elated to be alive.

During Cal's visit, he shocked me with the news that Vernon, knocked unconscious by the fall after Lobo's charge, had drowned in the Serpentine. Lobo must have left him to rescue me.

Yesterday Sut told me of the quiet, family funeral for Vernon, and also some details of the report he and Cal had made to the sheriff. When Lobo ran into the hideaway still wet from my rescue, Cal could tell that he'd come for help and followed the big animal to me. Cal had found Vernon's body, face down in shallow water. Cal had sent Lobo on ahead to K2 and had led Vernon's horse back at the same time he'd brought me in.

Bernie'd retrieved Jasper. Unlike Lobo, my good horse had missed the action.

As we left the hospital, Neva and Uncle Harry took turns talking, leaving me little chance to comment. I enjoyed hearing Neva tell of Lobo's return.

Neva, who had just driven out to the ranch that afternoon, had known Lobo was still alive. She wasn't surprised when he came running back into the K2 farmyard, but everyone else, thinking him dead, made quite a fuss over his return.

"Casey," she began, "You would have enjoyed all the happy reactions at seeing Lobo again. The ranch hands gathered around him, and Bernie actually knelt down and hugged him, while Stella came running out with a pan of table scraps."

"Now, Casey," Uncle Harry began. "If you feel up to it, I'm taking you to Seattle. I've arranged for someone to take over my superintendent's office while I'm away. He got off the train today from St. Paul; a Mr. Dean Smith."

Attempting to be cheerful, Uncle Harry smiled at me. "So Dean Smith will stay here while I go with Casey Jones. Heh heh, Smith and Jones, such uncommon names."

I laughed a little and Neva broke in. "It's good to hear you laugh again, Casey, after all you've been through."

"Well, now," I contrived, "It's been a rough time, but on the bright side, the sore spots are getting well. Even my shoulder is healing."

"I like your up-beat spirit, Casey." Uncle Harry said. "And I'm counting on the doctor in Seattle. I hear Dr. Kraft's the best ophthalmologist in the northwest. He'll help that banged-up left eye of yours see if anyone can."

As we walked, I recalled more details. I'd been rushed to the hospital from K2, I remember getting a shot for pain and the strange experience of having the doctor take four stitches as he sewed up the cut along the side of my nose.

The nurse let Lobo sit by my bed. It was such a comfort to have him there. Once he licked my face as I talked to him: "Thanks, ol' pal. You did it again for me out there, pushing me to the surface so I could swim to shore, then getting Cal to help . . . you're like my guardian angel."

When we climbed into the Ford, I gazed out west to the distant hills. Soon I'd be traveling out to them and beyond. I hoped to get my eye fixed, but that horizon beckoned with the promise of more adventure. I felt a sudden eagerness to quit this place and seek out new surroundings. So what if I'd have to work in a Seattle shop slicing smelly fish. I wanted to get away from the pain and, ugh! . . . the dark thoughts of Vernon.

I'd miss romping with Lobo and riding Jasper, but I'll get to attend high school again and read! How I longed to choose an interesting book, and I savored the thought of getting lost in reading it! I longed to explore the world beyond!

Back at the dinner table I got a shower of sparkling comments. But Aunt Louise summed it up nicely. "Casey, I'm sure we're all delighted at having you back with us. Though you've been here just a few weeks, we love you as a true member of our family."

Annie added, "Yes! Casey, you're better than a brother!" Colette insisted, "Mom's right, we sure missed you."

Neva reached over and squeezed my hand with a "Welcome back."

What a happy time for me! The blush on my face matched the red of the scars on my cheek. I looked around the table at each smiling face. "Thanks, you have made me feel at home here."

Aunt Louise served roast turkey, stuffing, mashed potatoes, with several savory side dishes as a special thanksgiving for my making a comeback. Helping myself to the feast, I lightened things up. "Aunt Louise, the turkey's delicious, but if you don't mind, I'll skip the horse-radish." Everyone chuckled, but Neva told me later that she had to laugh to keep from crying.

I noticed Olga Boltus smiling at my comment. How could she smile? Her dead son had almost killed me.

Then she answered my silent question. "Casey, when you first came to us, I hoped my Vernon might straighten himself out. But neither my pleading with him nor my mother's prayers would turn him from his obsession and hatred. Believe me, Casey, I did what I could to persuade him to change his ways. I'm ashamed that a son of mine would turn out so badly. Please accept my deep regret for your ordeal at Vernon's hands."

In reply, I reached across the table and took her hand. Tears rolled down her face and she dabbed them with her kerchief. "One more thing, Casey." She said. "You're a very fine person to make light of your being almost dragged to death with that little horseradish comment. In a way, I feel you're like a son to me."

The next morning at ten thirty-five, Uncle Harry and I stood on the railroad platform at the spot where we'd first met. As we waited for the westbound train, I thought of the nickel that I'd had in hand when he'd pulled me from the train. The coin had slipped away when Uncle Harry grabbed my arm. I looked down by the tracks that ran in front of where we stood.

"Uncle Harry," I began. "That day when I got off the train, I lost a nickel right about here."

"I'll help you look for it. It might be on the other side. "Yes, here it is, Casey."

Uncle Harry picked up the nickel and, with a broad grin, handed it to me. "It must have landed on the track. The train ran over it. It's been rolled out, bigger in size, but paper thin."

I took the coin and looked in amazement. I could still see

the image of a buffalo and read the inscription: "In God We Trust."

I slipped it my pocket as a memento of my time here.

Just then, a wagon with the rest of the family drove up to the curb. My cousins jumped out with the happy chatter and delightful giggles I'd come to expect from the three pretty girls. Even with one eye and my banged-up condition, they made me feel good, as always. I felt a special kind of love for all three of these happy girls. Bright, cheerful and caring, they had become more than cousins to me. Drawn to Annie, who went from serious to flippant in a blink, attracted to Colette so quick with a pretty smile and a hug, and with a deep fondness for no nonsense Neva, oh, how I would miss them!

Back when my train had chugged out of New York's Grand Central Station, my life had started rolling at a swift pace and hadn't slowed a bit. Now I looked down the track and saw my train as a speck in the distance. Soon I would continue my journey to Seattle and Aunt Minnie.

I received the best send-off I could imagine as my train approached. Aunt Louise took my hand, wished me well, and gave me a letter to her sister-in-law, Minnie. The girls each gave me a big hug and Colette kissed me on the cheek, while giving me her well-wishes. Even Mrs. Boltus had kind words and gave me a little package, with the words, "for you to enjoy on the trip."

Uncle Harry took over. "I checked our luggage, Casey. We have nothing to carry on with us." As he spoke, I wasn't supposed to overhear the girls' whispered comments, "Casey is just so good looking," came from Colette. "Yes, even with the scars, he's handsome," added Annie. "He seems so gown-up now!" Neva commented. "I pray that the doctor will heal his eye quickly so he can come right back to us."

Suddenly, I noticed the station agent hurrying toward us.

His face contorted, he had a wild look in his eye. "Mr. Kinsman!" he shouted. "There's been a terrible accident!" When he got close to us, he reported, "Ben, the brakeman on the switch engine, has been run down. He's dead. Backed over by the line of cars he was switching on the siding. Musta stepped between the rails with his back turned while checking his list."

Uncle Harry said, "Call the mortician to get him out of there. I'll be right with you!"

With deep concern, Uncle Harry looked at me. "Casey, you'll have to go on alone. I must go over and break the news to the man's widow. I'll try to get away and follow you in a day or two. In the meantime, explain things to your Aunt Minnie and Uncle Carl. I'll send her a telegram with the instructions about taking you to Dr. Kraft."

"Yes sir," I replied. "I understand, sir."

"I have to leave right now. Here is your pass to Seattle and the claim checks for our bags. Keep mine for me." Uncle Harry grabbed me by the shoulders. "You'll be all right, I'm sure."

As we parted he pressed a letter into my hand. "And, here, this letter came today from your mother." The next moment, the huge engine pulling my train thundered by in a storm of steam and cinders. Minutes later, settled to my seat, I waved to the Kinsman throng on the platform as the train pulled out. A wave of depression hit me as once again I watched the countryside roll by.

First, leaving my mother behind in New York and now my newly found family here reminded me of a boxer getting a one-two punch. Eagerly, I opened the letter from my mom.

Dear Casey,

Recently I've had to sell most of the furniture and move into a smaller apartment.

Your letters have been a great consolation for me.

Yes, your Uncle Harry got my permission to take you, for a

while at least, and Aunt Minnie found out at the same time.

It truly raises my spirits to think of you getting along so well with Harry, Louise and the girls. I grew up at Overton Manor, and have very pleasant memories of it and the K2 ranch. In my next letter, I'll provide details of my childhood.

I have a nice job in the ribbons and sundries counter at Clariges department store, so rest easy about me. I'm getting along all right, except that I do miss you, your dad and the happy life we once had.

Yes, perhaps some day I too can travel out west and we can be together again . . . at least for a visit.

Until then, my dear son, I know you will make your way in your new surroundings, while earning the respect of others.

With love always,

Your mother.

nineteen

VERNON'S VICTORY

I carefully placed Mom's letter in my jacket pocket, heaved a sigh and tried to clear my mind. I struggled to jack up my mood by thinking of the good times I'd had with the Kinsman family. The faces of so many kind people moved before me, against the backdrop of green fields that passed by outside my train window. I thought of Cal, who had saved my life with his native skills, of Bernie and Stella and, yes, even Sut who turned out to be a friend.

I thought of Lobo, the beautiful blue-eyed animal who'd saved my life and loved being at my side. At the thought of Jasper, my heart ached. It all seemed more than I could bear. I shook my head, longing for the feel of my fine horse under me. Suddenly, all senses alive, I re-lived loping out in the glowing cool of sunrise; the prairie alive with the earthy scents of sage mingled with dew on bunch grass; the distant cry of the hawk floated faintly from the hills. I never knew how much a human being could love a horse! I found myself thinking, "When others come and saddle you up, Jasper, do you miss me too?"

But the thought of Neva brought the deepest longing. I loved the rides in the wagon with her, and the swimming lessons. She, more than any other, had cheered me when I felt low.

Try as I would, I couldn't avoid thinking of Vernon. Maybe because I tried so hard not to think of him, the opposite happened. His face loomed before me. My brain seems not always to take directions. The more I tried to push Vernon from my mind, the more forcefully thoughts of him jumped to the surface. To make things worse, my train entered a tunnel. Now, with only blackness beyond the window, Vernon's smirking face loomed before me. I could even hear him say: "At last! I'm rid of you, City Boy!"

In an effort to escape the terrible vision, I turned, ready to jump from my seat, but could not. Someone blocked the way.

"Ticket please." The conductor stood in the aisle, and held out his hand.

I fumbled in my pocket and produced my railroad pass, as we roared out of the tunnel in bright sunlight again. I sat shaking. An awful thought froze me to my seat.

A voice inside shouted, "Oh my God! I fought the good fight, but Vernon won!"

Despite my prayers, pain and suffering, I'm on a train heading away from the family I had come to love. He'd forced me to leave. Would I ever return?

I strode through the aisle, trying to walk off my glum mood; I came to the last car, passed through the door, and stood outside. I hung onto the metal handrail watching the rugged countryside and, with it, the life I'd come to love, rapidly moving away. We'd left cottonwoods on low hills behind. Now I could smell the pleasant scent of the mountain pine and fir.

As we ascended the slopes of the Cascade Range, the change of scene helped to lighten my mood. A calm of sorts filled my heart and soothed my stomach. I took several deep breaths of sweet air and stared at the frothy clouds above. This afternoon I'd be with Aunt Minnie in Seattle. Needing to renew my resolve, I prayed, "Dear God, help me with this next big step in my life."

Hunger hit as I returned to my seat. I opened the package from Olga Boltus. Roast turkey between slices of home-made bread made my mouth water. I got a cup of coffee from the porter, and soon demolished the sandwiches and four ginger cookies as well. Then I felt something else in the bottom of the package. Thrusting my hand in, I happily brought out two big candy bars, plump peanuts in rich chocolate, my favorite. I thought of the flattened nickel in my pocket that I'd intended to spend for one of these bars. Now I had two bars and a souvenir nickel. Still, not much to show for what I'd been through back there.

I thought: "Thanks, Olga, I'm glad we made our peace before I left." Then, as I snuggled into my seat, I knew peace of mind. I took a big bite of candy. I'd replaced dark thoughts of Vernon with a pleasant one of his mother. Relaxed now, I slowly savored each bite of candy until it was gone.

twenty

SEATTLE AT LAST!

AUNT MINNIE

The train lurched to a stop. I jostled with the other passengers and jumped off, eager to find my aunt. I searched the platform for a middle-aged woman about the size of my mother. Surely Aunt Minnie would be looking for me: Uncle Harry had set everything up with her. Now I walked down the busy platform teeming with travelers and freight wagons, into the huge King Street Station, filled with people milling about or sitting on heavy wooden benches. The excitement I'd known earlier turned to worry. In his haste, Uncle Harry hadn't given me any money. My flattened nickel wouldn't buy much in the big city. I spent half an hour looking for Aunt Minnie with no success.

I'd begun to panic when someone touched me on the elbow. "Casey? Casey Jones?"

I turned to see a fine-looking woman with a tall man standing behind her.

"Yes! I'm Casey Jones. Are you Aunt Minnie?"

She hugged me and exclaimed, "Carl! I told you he'd be the one!"

The man moved forward and grasped my hand, shaking it

vigorously. "Glad to meet you, Casey Jones, very glad indeed! I'm your Uncle Carl Coleman. We were getting very worried about you . . . thought sure you'd not arrived as planned . . . for the second time in a month."

"How do you do, sir," I answered. "And I'm happy to meet you too, Aunt Minnie."

Aunt Minnie wore a big lavender hat with feathers, and gloves to match. Her pretty brown eyes sparkled, and I noticed her perfume when she gave me a hug. She took my hand with a big smile and said, "Welcome to Seattle, Casey. I simply can't tell you how happy I am you're here safe and sound!"

Uncle Carl asked, "Why are you alone, Casey? We expected Harry Kinsman to be with you."

In a few words I explained about his last-minute emergency in Arborville, and I went with Uncle Carl to pick up the luggage, including Uncle Harry's bag. Meanwhile, Aunt Minnie stopped at the Western Union desk, where she sent a telegram to the Kinsmans letting them know I'd arrived safely. Then we were off in a spiffy Packard roadster, dodging downtown traffic.

Happy to be traveling city streets again, and surprised at Seattle's tall buildings, I noticed the smell of the salt-water harbor as I caught glimpses of the waterfront. Some parts of the city matched areas of New York with the bustle of wagons and automobiles, people hurrying to cross paved streets, and shops and businesses everywhere. But Seattle wasn't flat. We swooped up hills at every turn until, miles later, we came to a very nice, tree-lined avenue and parked below an eight-story building.

We took the elevator to the top floor, and Aunt Minnie and Uncle Karl ushered me into their beautiful apartment. I made my way to a large picture window. The view of the bay and snow-covered mountains beyond took my breath away.

I turned and noted some of the most beautiful living-room furniture I'd ever seen. Then, the smiling couple showed me to my room. In its own way, with a nice but plain bed, dresser and desk, it suited me just right. I instantly felt at home here. From the window behind the desk, I gazed below and noticed a city park across the street. So far, I liked Seattle and the Colemans too.

At dinner I learned that there were no Coleman children, so the three of us enjoyed a meal of pork chops, baked potatoes and a tossed salad. Mixed in the salad was a soft, tasty green vegetable I never had before. Aunt Minnie laughed pleasantly when I asked her about it.

"Avocado, Casey, I've mixed in some California avocado." She brought a whole one from the ice-box and handed it to me. Its rough, dark skin didn't appeal to me, but inside it was deliciously smooth and mellow.

After dinner, we relaxed in the living room over coffee. I sank into a big chocolate-colored chair and thought, "This is true comfort."

"We do love it here in Seattle, Casey," said Aunt Min, now settled in to her soft, wing chair. "And we're so pleased that now, at last, you are with us."

Uncle Carl's gray eyes twinkled. "Yes, and we intend to make your stay a pleasant one. What did you think of the train ride? Was it clear enough to see the higher elevations of the Cascade Mountains as you came over them?"

"I did get a glimpse of some high, snow-capped peaks. The whole range seems mighty impressive . . . like the Rocky Mountains I crossed the day before my train got to Arborville."

"I see . . . no big surprise for you then. But did you expect to see the Olympic Mountains out there on our western horizon?"

"Now that was a huge surprise! When I gazed out at that

snow-covered splendor for the first time, I'd never before seen anything quite so spectacular."

Uncle Carl gestured toward the large window. "Well, we do enjoy our Pacific Northwest scenery."

"And nearby, Seattle has beautiful Lake Washington just to the east, and down below, Lake Union," added Aunt Min.

"Skidoo! Mountains, lakes, rivers, forests . . . when I got on the train to come here, I certainly didn't imagine all this."

Uncle Carl's chest seemed to swell with pride. "All these gifts of nature may be somewhat overwhelming at first, but just wait 'til tomorrow. If it's a clear day, you will see the crown jewel, Mount Rainier. It dominates this whole area with its pristine elegance."

Too overcome for words, I peered out at the gorgeous sunset as rose and gold shafts of light spread in radiance across the sky.

Then Uncle Carl lit a long cigar and frowned at me.

"Casey, I wish to explain why we didn't come up to you right away at the train station. We expected Harry would be with you. Then, too, he hadn't mentioned your eye patch in his telegram, just that he'd secured an appointment with a Seattle doctor for you."

Aunt Minnie leaned forward. "Casey, have you been in a fight?"

I smiled and said simply that I'd been dragged by a horse.

The Colemans seemed shocked, but relieved. Uncle Carl's pleasant smile returned. "Well now, that's quite understandable, Casey. It takes a while to learn horsemanship. Have you recovered in other ways?"

"You may have noticed the scabs on my face. Yes, I'm healing nicely. But I hope that a Dr. Kraft here in Seattle can help my injured eye."

Uncle Carl seemed relieved. "Dr. Kraft! We didn't know

the name of the doctor. First thing tomorrow, we'll find out the time of your appointment."

Aunt Minnie sat beside me. "Casey, in the letter you brought from Louise, she mentioned school. Would you like to enter high school?"

I couldn't hide my feelings. "Yes! Yes, I would. Can I go to school here while my eye is healing?"

"You certainly can. You have been enrolled at Noah Webster High since your mother first arranged for you to stay with us. The principal has received your transcript from New York, and the school is only four blocks from this apartment."

"Skidoo! That's really great! When does fall term begin?"

"It began yesterday, Casey. We phoned the office. You can make up the first day or two."

That settled, Aunt Minnie asked about Mom. The evening passed quickly as I went into some detail about my dad's last days and the decision to send me away to live. We decided to get a good night's sleep, because the next day promised to be full, but before I rolled into bed, I wrote Mom a note. I described my welcome and how the kindness I'd received had prompted warm feelings. I'd tell her about my eye injury later.

The very next day, I had my appointment with Dr. Kraft. Aunt Minnie sat with me in the waiting room located in a downtown building.

I felt the patch over my eye. The swelling seemed to be almost gone and hair had grown back, partly hiding the gash on my scalp. My stomach growled some, in anticipation, but the oatmeal and raisin breakfast set well as the door to the inner office opened and my name was called.

Aunt Min came in with me, I shook hands with Dr. Kraft, a stocky man of about fifty with a crop of black hair, but no beard or mustache.

"Hello, there, young man," he said cheerfully. "So we have

a problem eye, do we."

Moments later he'd removed the patch from my left eye. He flashed a bright light in first one, then the other, eye. Then he gave his attention to the left one.

"Have you injured this eye before, Casey?"

"Yes sir. I had some slivers removed from it three years ago after a piece of wood had flipped into it."

"That explains the small scars I note on your retina."

He covered my right eye: "Can you see my hand?"

"Yes."

"How many fingers can you see?"

"Four. But they're blurry."

"Casey, I find no permanent injury. Your eye appears to be healing from the blow it received. Hopefully, in a week or so, clear vision will return."

"All right! I hoped you'd say that."

"I'll give you some eye drops, and for the next three or four days, continue to protect it with the eye patch. Come back in a week and we'll have another look at it."

That evening during the family chat time, Uncle Carl asked, "Would you like to see our fish processing operation?"

"I would. Is it anything like the Fulton Fish Market?"

Both aunt and uncle laughed heartily, then Uncle Carl answered, "No, nothing like it. At Coleman Industries, we put fish in tin cans, mostly salmon."

"Can it?"

"Yes, our processing plant is on the waterfront. Fisherman bring in boat-loads of fish to us."

I stopped to consider that. I had imagined a small shop, where people came in, bought a pound or so of sea-food, and took it home for dinner. Canning fish would be a big operation.

Uncle Carl went on. "We weigh the catch, buy it, and process it. Of the three operations, which one would you think would be the most exacting, the step that absolutely must run smoothly with no mistakes?

I answered immediately, "Getting an accurate weight of the catch."

Uncle Carl sat back in his chair; a smile slowly spread across his face. He replied: "Ummm." Uncle Carl seemed to enjoy my answer as much as his after-dinner brandy.

"Min, what did I tell you. This young man is sharp as a slicing knife."

Aunt Minnie beamed. "Well, Casey, you gave the right answer, now enlarge on it. Why is the job of getting an exact weight of the fish so important to our business?"

Happy to have said the right thing, I went on. "Because any little mistake could cause a problem with the fishermen on one hand, or result in a loss of profit for us on the other."

My face got red when I realized that, in response to Aunt Min, I'd said, "us," thus including myself as part of the company. I hadn't even seen the cannery and I sounded like a part-owner.

I tried to make up for it with, "I meant to say loss for the company."

Uncle Carl's eyes sparkled and he laughed again. "Casey, you're a good kid! I've taken a liking to you right off. Don't feel that you mis-spoke. Actually, you can be a part of our family's enterprise. And, as for your answer, you show an amazing grasp of the situation; spoken like a true Kinsman, wouldn't you say, Min!"

"You are indeed my sister's son, Casey. Tomorrow you start school, but we'll find a way to get you down to the waterfront too."

Uncle Carl took a small wallet from his jacket. "We received a telegram from your Uncle Harry who forgot to give you some spending money. "Here, Casey take this."

    Startled and pleased, I accepted ten one dollar bills with a, "Thank you sir."

twenty-one

WEBSTER HIGH INITIATION

I'll always remember August 25th as the day I first met Sniggy Jacobs. He and his two pals routinely gave new kids a bad time.

Sniggy stood in Webster High's hallway snickering, hair slicked back with Macassar oil. He imagined, I supposed, that its black gleam attracted the girls. As his small eyes shone with malice, he announced to his cronies, "Just wait 'til that sheenie kid from New York comes out of the office, we'll give him a razzing!"

Buddy Flipton and Perry Yowts, his pals, sneered as they kicked small beanbags against the corridor wall with the heels of their yellow, leather shoes.

"Yeah, Sniggy," said Perry, also known as Chisel, due to his buck teeth. "We'll give 'em the ol' squeeze play in the hall."

Just then, I charged out of the office, looking for the location of my first classroom. Buddy whispered, "Heads up! This must be the sissy comin' now."

At first, the three, surprised at my appearance, hesitated to put their violent plan into action. They had expected a baby-faced boy in neat jacket and knickers. Instead, I came at them in a cowboy shirt and denim pants from the K2 ranch. The eye-patch, facial scabs and serious expression gave me a look more like Billy the Kid on his way to shooting up a saloon.

But with a whispered, "let's go," from Sniggy, the three moved to execute the squeeze play. Buddy walked along on my right and Chisel fell in on my left, with Sniggy close behind. As we turned the corner, out of sight of those in the main hallway, Buddy stepped in front of me, and opened a heavy, wooden closet door. Chisel on my left and Sniggy from behind intended to smash me into the door, lock me into the closet, and leave me there for the janitor to find.

I'd begun to navigate with one eye by turning my head slightly from side to side. That, coupled with a sideways eye motion, gave me a fraction of a second's warning. Just as when riding Jasper, I'd seen Sut's rope coming, now I reacted to Buddy reaching in front of me. I darted to my left. When Sniggy hit me from behind, instead of my face smashing flat, full force into the heavy door, only my arm caught the edge of it, causing me to spin past Buddy and hit the opposite wall with my injured left shoulder. I staggered back, trying to gauge exactly what had happened.

At first I couldn't believe I'd been purposely attacked. But when I saw the sneering faces of the three, I knew I'd received the "new boy" treatment. Then, Sniggy pushed by me with such force I bounced off the wall again, but remained standing as all three of the rowdies disappeared around the corner.

Another boy picked up my notebook. "You just dodged a bullet." He said. "Here, when you hit the door, this went flying."

Holding my shoulder, I reached for my notebook. "Thanks. I should have expected something like this on my first day."

"Yes, it happens every August to unlucky guys. New girls just get ignored, but for a new guy, it can get rough. Last year,

Sniggy and his gang did the 'open door in the face' thing and the new kid spent his first morning in the broom closet."

"Well, I guess it could have been worse then."

"Yeah, they're the meanest kids in this part of town. But I might help some, if you want . . . I'm Gene Clodell and you are Casey Jones. I heard you were coming." Then he smiled with only half of his face and added, "Wrecked any trains lately?"

I chuckled at that. "Right now I'm sort of a wreck myself, but I got banged up by a horse, not a locomotive."

"Yeah, I just noticed your shoulder is bleeding through your shirt. I guess you didn't get off scot-free from Sniggy's welcome."

"Yeah, Gene. Glad to have someone friendly just now. Show me the nearest boy's room, will ya? I need to check out this shoulder."

Five minutes later, after I'd borrowed Gene's handkerchief for a quick bandage, I entered the science classroom that Gene pointed out to me. So far, in my first day of school since I'd left Brooklyn, I'd re-injured my shoulder and made a new friend. Now, from my secure desk by the windows, I looked around. I was impressed by what I saw. The kids looked nice, and I felt no Brooklyn school would have had better science materials. Color charts covered the walls depicting everything from animals to volcanoes, from insects to the solar system, and in back stood a huge, well-stocked aquarium.

This first-period class, general science, would be divided into two parts for the year. First semester covered natural science, the earth and the planets. Next would come the study of plants and animals. The subject matter and the excellent textbook, filled with diagrams and color photos, couldn't have pleased me more. Then I really got excited as I began to know the teacher. Young, with the look of a distance runner, Mr. Drake's voice and friendly brown eyes gave me confidence.

"Welcome, Casey. These next few weeks we'll learn mostly about our sun and the planets. See me after class for the first two days' assignments."

Mr. Drake pulled down a chart of our solar system and kept everyone's interest for the entire period with his lecture on the sun's effect on the earth.

Gene was waiting for me in the hall afterwards and guided me to my next class.

"Say, Casey. Mind my asking about your eye patch? Were you thrown from a horse?"

"Not exactly. It's a long story . . . maybe over lunch."

Later Gene and I had so many other things to chat about, classes, girls, and teachers, my past didn't come up. As our friendship grew, I knew we'd have time to catch up on the personal stuff.

Gene and I had fourth-period English class together, and the rest of the afternoon went smoothly. I couldn't let my first day go by without seeing the rather large library, the size of two classrooms. I got a good first look around, but postponed a closer investigation until I could do it justice.

twenty-two

WATERFRONT CRISIS

UNCLE CARL

School let out at 3:00. I sprinted up the hill to my new home, where Aunt Min met me at the door, full of questions about how things had gone for me on the first day. I painted a positive picture, including how Mr. Drake and the other teachers had worked me right into their classes. I didn't mention getting roughed up in the hallway.

As I changed into more comfortable clothes, I put a new bandage on my painful shoulder. A depressing thought surfaced: "Gee, with Arborville behind me, I figured I'd left threats and violence behind. Instead I get waylaid on my first day in a Seattle school."

On impulse, I rid myself of one negative reminder. I took off the eye patch. I thought, "There! Even with blurred sight, I feel better now."

Trying to be up-beat, I told Aunt Min about Gene; how he'd "showed me the ropes." Using a nautical term seemed appropriate.

"Hmm, made a friend on the first day? That's excellent. You'll have interesting things to write to your mother."

"I will. It should make Mom glad."

Then, right off, Aunt Min announced that we were leaving for the waterfront.

"It's only 3:30. We can meet your Uncle Carl before the next shift begins at the shop."

Minutes later, we arrived at a large building set on pilings over the water. I liked the salt-water smell of things. The sights and sounds reminded me of lower Manhattan.

Ferryboats crisscrossed the bay, slipping past huge steamships plying the vast inland waterway route to the ocean. Raised near New York harbor, one of the busiest ports in the world, I still got a thrill from being on Seattle's teeming waterfront. As I stood on the wharf, I saw ships from the seven seas flying the flags of far-flung countries.

Beyond the harbor, a tugboat busily herded a raft of several hundred logs to a waiting sawmill on up the bay. What a busy place!

Aunt Min left to do some shopping after Uncle Carl met us outside his office. He pointed at two fishing boats out in the bay. "Look there!" he called out over the noise of the cannery behind us. "They're racing each other to be the first to unload their catch at our dock."

Uncle Carl turned to me. "Glad you're here, Casey. You're in time to see the change of shift. The day crew begins work at 9:00 in the morning when the first boats arrive, and works to 5:00 when the evening shift begins. It runs until we finish canning the day's catch . . . usually about 1:00 or 2:00 in the morning."

I looked down on the main floor from our catwalk position just outside the office. Fifty or so workers were busily involved cleaning and slicing salmon into pieces that would be put into cans by others down the line. Then a machine topped off the cans with water and sealed them with a metal lid. Uncle Carl pointed ahead to the next step, where the cans in metal trays were stacked on carts, then rolled into one end of big cylinders with a 7-foot opening at one end.

"Those are the retorts," Uncle Carl explained. "They are steam pressure cookers. We have four of them, each like a big can itself, lying on its side. When they are filled with canned fish on the carts, we close the retort door, seal it, and run steam inside. That cooking step takes about an hour. Then we cut the steam and fill the retort with water to cool it."

I asked, "While the salmon is being cooked, why doesn't the sealed can bulge out or burst?"

"Good question, Casey. A lot of folks that tour the plant ask that question. The answer is that the pressures inside and outside the can remain the same."

"O.K., that explains it. But now what about the most important part of the processing plant?"

Uncle Carl smiled. "Glad you hadn't forgotten our earlier mention of the weighing-in step. I've saved that for last. Follow me down below."

We moved to a shed attached to the main building on the unloading dock. A fishing boat had pulled alongside, and four men were forking salmon into carts.

"The salmon in those carts are Seattle's pride. Each fish weighs 40 or 50 pounds. A full cart will have at least 1000 pounds of fish inside," said Uncle Carl, bragging a little.

"Skidoo! That's a lot of salmon!"

I watched as a clerk carefully recorded the weight shown on the scale. The fish were dumped onto a conveyor belt that took them inside the main building. Within minutes they would be inside a can.

The scale consisted of a platform and a metal post with a large, round face on it that showed weights up to 2000 pounds. As I watched, a cart filled with salmon being weighed a big pointer, like a clock hand, swung around and stopped just past the number 1061.

The clerk sang out: "A thousand sixty one and five ounces."

Uncle Carl seemed pleased to announce, "We pay two cents a pound for salmon."

Two cents didn't seem like a lot to me, but then, I remembered that a one-pound can of salmon cost only twenty cents at the grocery store. Impressed, I pondered the importance of providing a nutritious main dish, that even the poorest family could afford.

I was eager to find out more about the busy cannery, so I asked questions and walked around with Uncle Carl, for another hour. I got to see over a hundred workers on the floor as the next shift took over.

Back in the office, I sat looking around at Uncle Carl's nicely furnished office, his big desk, the pictures of fishing boats on the walls, and a shelf with a model boat that featured an actual ship's compass.

I asked, "Uncle Carl, are you the sole owner, or are there partners?"

"I'm the majority stock holder and manager of Coleman Canning Corporation. We employ 120 men and women during the salmon run, and 25 in the off-season."

"I'm really impressed, Uncle Carl. When Mom told me I'd be coming out here, I had no idea what to expect."

"Thought we might be a small retail shop on the edge of town?"

"Well, yes, I pictured myself wielding a slicing knife at a fish counter . . . you know, like at the Fulton Fish Market."

Uncle Carl got a really good laugh at that. "Ah yes. The Fulton Fish Market. I've been there. Quite a lot of fish go through it. But we're different, as you can see."

Uncle Carl ran his fingers through his wiry blond hair.

His usual positive expression changed. "Casey, we must make enough through the sale of our canned salmon to pay all our expenses. This year we are barely doing that, even though nothing has changed from last year."

I thought of the scale operation.

"I know the problem must be at the weigh-in, we're recording more fish than we actually can. Somehow the weight of the fish is being padded."

I stepped to the window that looked down on the scale. "Uncle Carl, I noticed a small telescope on the shelf up there by your boat model. May I use it for a minute?"

"Sure, Casey."

I walked to the window, and picked up a pad and paper on the way. With the telescope I could see the weight of each cartfull, as the black hand circled around and pointed to a number that indicated the weight. I quickly set down the amount on the pad. I did this for the next four times a cart rolled onto the platform, then I handed the pad to Uncle Carl. "Would this be a way to check on the man who is doing the weigh-in?"

"Yes, by Jove! Why didn't I think of it? It's so simple, and yet exact. The next time a boat pulls up, we will record the weights of the cart loads of fish from it, and match our figures with what is turned in from our man down there."

Minutes later, the next boat pulled in, loaded with the day's catch. "That's Mike Elioto's boat. A very good family man."

Uncle Carl peered through the telescope and called out the weights from the scale as I wrote them down. When Uncle Carl totaled the weight, it came to 14,537 pounds 9 ounces.

"That's the weight of the car and the fish together. The cart weighs exactly 300 pounds and there were 11 cart loads weighed, so we subtract 3300 from the total. That's 11,237 pounds 9 ounces of fish for Mike Elioto's catch, for which we'll pay him $224.75."

"I'll wait 'til the end of the shift to get the weight from down there. If I asked for it now, it might arouse suspicion."

Aunt Min arrived soon after, and we were on our way back to the apartment.

"Did you find your tour of the cannery interesting?" she asked.

"Did I ever! I saw a thousand things I'd never seen before. Then, Uncle Carl posed a problem and asked for my help to solve it."

"I know the problem he mentioned to you," Aunt Min replied. "Carl must solve this problem or Coleman Cannery will go out of business. Over a hundred people will lose their jobs and the fishermen will have to find another way to sell the fish they catch."

"Did Uncle Carl say he suspects the weight of the fish is being padded somehow?"

"Yes. Before he talked to you about it, I'm the only other person he's confided in. Carl suspects the man who is the weigh-master on the second shift. His name is Clodell, Donovan Clodell."

"C-Clo-dell?" I stuttered.

"Yes, he and his family live just a few blocks from here."

"Aunt Min! The friend I met today at school is named, Gene Clodell!"

twenty-three

THE MYSTERIOUS PHANTOM FISH

When Uncle Carl arrived home last evening, he came to my room.

"Casey, I got the tally for that catch we checked on. It's exact to the ounce. The weigh-master did a perfect job."

"Well, that helps to clear Mr. Clodell and the other weigh-masters. Uncle Carl, I think the problem lies somewhere else."

Uncle Carl looked haggard. "I'll level with you, Casey. We only have a week to solve this mystery of the missing salmon. At the end of the month we'll have to declare bankruptcy and close."

The next day at school, much relieved at not seeing Sniggy or his buddies, I warmed up to the routine. I still had to sit out the flag football, watching Gene and the other guys enjoying their physical activity. Other than a sore shoulder, I felt fine.

On our way back from the field, Gene and I struck up a conversation. "I like your looks better without the eye patch," Gene confided. "Yesterday you reminded me of Black Bart the Pirate."

"I've felt more like a tornado victim, but in another few

days I'll be fit as a fisherman."

"When the eye doctor is finished with you, are you going back to Arborville?"

"That's the plan, but I think I'll be around 'til the end of the school term, anyway. In the meantime, I'd sure like to help with the mystery down at the cannery."

Gene needed to shower so we headed across the lawn toward the gym. I wondered if my comment would get a reaction. It did. Gene stopped and stared at me.

"What mystery?" he asked guardedly.

"Gene, I'm not supposed to talk about it, but I need your help."

Gene frowned and said simply, "Go on."

"I overheard Uncle Carl say that even though sales are up compared to last year, the cannery's profit is down."

Gene nodded and began to walk with me again. "What do you want from me?"

"Well, do you know your way around at the cannery? I think you and I might solve the mystery of the phantom fish."

"Phantom fish? What do you mean?"

I smiled, trying to lighten things up. "Before I say any more, Gene, are you with me or not."

"I don't get it." Gene sniffed. "You breeze in here from that hick town, Arborville, and in a week's time you're set to tell us how to run the biggest operation on the Seattle waterfront."

"Gene, can't you see? As an outsider, I might have an advantage working with you on this."

"Why, because you think my dad, as head weigh-master, might be involved in falsifying records?"

"No, Gene! Don't jump to the wrong conclusion. But sometimes those closest to the problem have trouble seeing the answer. You know, the old, 'can't see the forest for the trees,' thing. This is a weighty problem, no pun intended. We need to solve the mystery and save the cannery."

Gene, nodded, "O.K. you convinced me. What do you have in mind?"

"Now you're talking! Let's focus on facts."

"O.K., my dad is beside himself over the fact that somehow the tally is off and he feels it's his fault."

"Not if the weigh-in system's been rigged." I argued.

Gene stopped walking to make his point. "Dad says he starts his shift by checking the weight of the empty cart for accuracy, and the worker who pushes the full cart onto the scale steps back as it is being weighed . . . no chance for him to influence the weight with his foot."

"Gene, do you recall any changes in the weigh-in area with the last few months? Any repairs that would have allowed someone to cleverly modify the routine?"

Gene's eyes opened wide. "Yes, we replaced the platform planks under the rails the cart runs on. Water dripping from the fish had begun to rot them."

"That's it! Re-nailing the rails to new planks gave someone just the opportunity they needed to rig the system!"

Gene squinted with a puzzled expression. "I don't get it. When there's nothing on it, the platform, with its rails, balance out. The black hand on the scale points to zero. After the planks had been replaced, I saw an agent from the state department of weights and measures adjust the scale to the ounce. He even put an official seal on it to attest to its accuracy."

I had to admit that blasted my theory. "Well, Gene, while you shower, I'll think it over and meet you back here."

Just then, I looked up to see Sniggy and his two pals, Chisel and Buddy, approaching. Sniggy came right up to me. "Hey, Kid, you got lucky your first day. We usually give numb heads like you a real, fine welcome," he sneered. Sniggy needed a shower bad. I could smell his sweat, and his greasy hair shone in the sun.

Chisel glared at me with watery eyes. "Yeah, most new kids don't get off so easy, we still oughta initiate you right."

Buddy came so close I had to step back. He looked me in the eye. "So you took off your patch, eh. How'd you get hurt, in a fight?"

I chose my words carefully. "It happened in the woods."

All three laughed as they moved on. "Just what we need around here, a dumb back-woods yokel."

As Chisel moved away, he spat at my feet. "You're not off the hook yet, Rookie. One of these times we're gonna get you good."

The three gave me a case of bad feelings, like when I'd been Vernon's target, but I fought off the "downer," and Gene reappeared about the time I got my mind back to the mystery of the missing fish.

I picked up where we'd left off. "Gene, can you get us into the cannery? I think the next step is to examine the platform at the scale."

"The guard at the gate knows me. I can go and come as I want."

After school, we hopped a streetcar to the waterfront and, sure enough, the guard waved us through the gate. No problem there, but as we walked down to the scale, two burly fishermen ran over and threatened us.

With gray eyes flashing, one with curly red hair shouted, "Hey, you kids, get outa here!"

Another black-haired muscular man of action roared, "Someone's gonna get hurt!"

As we turned around and trotted down the wharf, he continued to shout, "Someone's gonna get hurt!"

I glanced over my shoulder as we clambered up the stairs. The men slowly turned and walked toward the Silver Belle, a large fishing boat moored at the wharf. Day-shift workers poured out of the exits and through the gate. "No swing shift today," observed Gene. "The plant will be closing for the day."

Gene and I mixed in with about fifty women who'd been cleaning and slicing, and several men from the retort area joined us as well. The odor of sweat mixed with a strong smell of salmon. I felt depressed by the knowledge that these good, hard-working people would soon be out of work.

As we left the cannery, a coffee shop came into view. A sign in the window read, HOMADE PIES. I thought of the expense money that Uncle Carl had given me. "Gene, let's have some pie and coffee while we talk things over. I'll buy."

"Sure, this place serves the best cherry pie I've ever tasted."

Forking down the pie, we mulled over our violent reception on the dock.

"The guy with red hair who shouted at us is Bin Dunn, also known as Snapper," Gene began. "He's captain of the Silver Belle. My dad says he gets into a brawl just about every Saturday night at that bar across the street, called The Anchor."

Just then, I spotted the red-headed captain through the window. "Skidoo! There's Snapper and his pals walking in over there right now. Tell me, Gene, why did they make such a big fuss when we walked down to the scale?"

Gene swallowed his last bite of pie and came back with, "Maybe they've jimmied the scale and don't want us nosing around. We might find out the secret of how they did it."

"Right! And while they're boozing it up across the street, we have a chance to get back to the wharf and look around."

We took a short-cut across the cannery's main floor, almost deserted now. We walked up to the scale, while cautiously surveying the area for hostile fisherman. The Silver Belle seemed deserted as she slowly rose and fell at her briny berth.

While Gene climbed into the cart to have a look, I peered underneath. I prayed we'd find the answer to the mystery that endangered the livelihood of not only the cannery workers, but the fishermen themselves, who might be in danger of killing the goose that lays the golden eggs for them.

I found two suspicious-looking wires attached to a metal device the size of a dinner plate. Up above, Gene exclaimed, "I think I've solved the mystery! Casey, look at this!"

I leaned over the edge of the cart and saw two large metal hooks mounted in the bottom. "See, these hooks are bent to one side, so they will keep a large salmon from sliding out when the cart is dumped. That means a 40- to 50-pound fish will go back, and be weighed over and over again."

"Gene, you found it! It's as simple as holding one fish back while the others move on."

While Gene clambered out of the cart, I calculated the cost of this clever method of cheating.

"Let's see now, we'll set the weight of a fish trapped in the cart at 40 pounds. On a busy day, a cart would be weighed and dumped 10 to 20 times for each boat's catch. Gene! That mounts up! Each boat would get paid for an extra 400 to 800 pounds of fish because of those hooks mounted in the bottom."

"Wow! No wonder the company's going broke."

Gene thought for a minute. "I'll bet that when the cart rolls back after the last weigh-in, someone uses one of those unloading forks to lift the salmon out of those hooks in the bottom of the cart. That salmon could then be sold to a restaurant or fish market."

"Let's get out of here, Gene. We got what we came for."

"Gee whizz, Casey! We did a neat piece of detective work today."

"Yeah." I quipped. "When my Uncle Carl hears about the stowaway fish, he's going to be happy as a horse in a hay pasture."

twenty-four

THE TURNAROUND

That night, I snuggled down in my comfortable bed, pleased with our day of detective work. Just before I dozed off, I thought of Gene's dad. My earlier sadness . . . imagining so many people being hit by the cannery's closing, now turned into deep contentment. Still, finding the hooks seemed such a simple thing . . . maybe too simple. A disturbing idea crept into my sleepy mind. What if those two wires I'd found attached to the metal object under the platform also played a part in the plot to pad the tally? By coincidence, just yesterday in science class, Mr. Drake had showed us how an electromagnet produced a strong magnetic field.

I sat up in bed. That's it! The hooks are only part of the answer. The fishermen from the Silver Belle probably put a magnet where it could pull down on the metal cart. When switched on, the scale would read extra pounds and more phantom fish would be credited to the fishermen. All the boats would get extra pay from the hooking device, but only one boat might benefit by activating the switch to the magnet. Very clever.

Earlier that evening, Aunt Min had cooked a special meal to celebrate, with a Baked Alaska for dessert. Uncle Carl had marched back and forth in the apartment, happily muttering to himself over and over: "We're going to make it after all." Then he stopped and turned to me.

"Casey, you and Gene have done it! The cannery will stay open. We owe you a great debt of thanks."

I turned over and fell asleep, thinking of the next morning, when I'd let Uncle Carl in on the rest of the mystery.

The hooks in the cart were removed and Gene's dad slid under the platform and snipped the wires for the electromagnet. The results of these two corrections immediately made a difference. By the end of day, with a steady stream of salmon from boats plying the Puget Sound to our cannery dock, it was all two shifts could do to keep up with the day's heavy catch – now weighed in accurately.

Uncle Carl worked around the clock. Up in the office with him, I'd helped monitor the scale with the telescope, to double-check the weigh-in for both shifts. At 2:30 in the morning, he put down the tally sheets with a broad smile. "Casey, I've confirmed it. When I attend the board of directors meeting next week, I can verify the fact that we will once again make a profit. I'm sure they will rescind the decision to close the cannery."

Uncle Carl went on to describe a meeting he'd had that evening with the man I knew as Red Snapper, the skipper of the Silver Belle. "When Donovan Clodell and I caught Bin Dunn flipping the magnet's switch as the cart weighed their fish, we had evidence of cheating. I threatened legal action unless he agreed to a pay-back plan. He did. For the rest of the season, he'll accept only a penny a pound for the Silver Belle's catch.

I mentioned that the pay-back would help off-set the loss, but not make up for all the boats getting a bonus from the re-weigh of salmon held back by the hooks.

"That's true, Casey. But all of this would be difficult to

prove in court. We just have to accept our past losses and go on from here. We're sending a letter to all the skippers of the boats. It simply describes the hooks in the cart. This will explain why their payments from us were up this year. We placed no blame for the hooks. We've mounted them on a piling where the fisherman can see them."

For several days, I'd had an idea in mind: "Uncle Carl, I noticed that the salmon heads and tails are thrown away. Back in Brooklyn, we learned that before the pilgrims celebrated the first Thanksgiving, Squanto, an Indian, showed them how to plant corn in mounds."

"Yes, I remember that story too."

"Then you might recall that Squanto taught the Pilgrims to plant a fish along with the seeds of corn for fertilizer."

"Fertilizer!" Uncle Carl said excitedly. "Yes. Fish make good fertilizer. Are you suggesting that we investigate the possibility of selling the waste parts of the salmon for agriculture?"

"It could be another way to make up for the lost income." I replied.

"It could, but we'd need investment money to develop a new project. Right now we have a low credit rating at the bank."

"Uncle Harry promised he'd visit over here to check on me. Maybe I could ask him if he'd be interested in a fertilizer project. The K2 ranch might be the first customer for fish fertilizer."

"Casey, you have a creative streak in you. You are a born businessman. Certainly. We can have a chat with your other uncle when he comes here to visit."

"One more thing about planning a possible fertilizer project. Wouldn't we have to cut and dry the fish waste?"

"Yes."

"Well, a machine could chop up the waste and maybe when we let the steam out of the retorts, we could heat the dryers with it."

"Yes, I can see a basic plan shaping up. Casey, I think your ideas have a potential for profit. I'll present it to our Board of Directors."

twenty-five

MIXED REACTION

The next day, on the way home, Gene, usually given to measured comments, hardly paused long enough for me to chime in. Our conversation bounced around like a bell-buoy out in the bay.

"Casey, last night Dad chattered all through dinner... clear 'til bedtime about how the two of us had solved the weigh-in mystery." Gene practically danced down the sidewalk. "Dad called us young heroes, and said we deserved a medal for staving off the cannery's shut-down. He said the word down on the floor spread to everybody. Most didn't even know how close they'd come to losing their jobs."

"I wonder if the part about the electromagnet is common knowledge, too."

"No. Dad said we should keep that quiet. It's part of the agreement we have with the crew of the Silver Belle," Gene continued. "But, Casey, speaking of the crew, Dad heard that 'Red Snapper' is really sore about getting caught using the magnet to cheat the scale."

"I'm not surprised."

"Yeah, but the word's going around that Red's out to get even with you."

"Just me?"

"Yeah. Everyone knows that I found the hooks, but only the crew of the Silver Belle know about you finding the magnet."

"So I guess I'd better be careful."

"Yeah, Dad thinks it best if you stay away from the cannery until things settle down about this weigh-in thing."

"I agree. I need to concentrate on my homework anyway."

Just as we turned up the street to go home, two girls from our class came up.

Gene called out, "Hi, Veronica. Hello, Janet."

"Hi, there, Gene," Veronica said cheerfully. "Have you two met Janet? She's new here, like you, Casey." I liked Janet, her light brown hair done in a pony-tail and her smiling eyes.

We greeted Janet, and she responded with, "Hello, Casey. What do you think of the big city, so far?"

"Hi, Janet. Seattle? There's a surprise waiting around every corner," I responded. "How about you?"

"My family comes from the flat land of North Dakota. I'm still getting used to the hills."

Veronica laughed. "Yeah, me too, and I've lived around here all my life." She wore her dark hair in one long braid, tied in back with a green ribbon. Her smile set off her attractive, rounded features as she went on. "Say, we've heard that you pulled off a big discovery down at the cannery."

"We got lucky," returned Gene modestly.

"Well, from what we've been hearing, it was smart detective work and a lot of workers owe you thanks for it," Janet retorted.

"While climbing around on the dock, Gene solved the

problem," I replied.

"Good for you, Gene," continued Veronica. "But, Casey, we also heard the rumor that Sniggy and his pals are out to get you."

Janet, with her beautiful look of concern, reminded me of Neva as she said, "Yes, Casey, you'd best be careful. I heard that even some of the teachers are intimidated by Sniggy's gang."

We exchanged a few more comments and then went our separate ways. But once again the heavy cloud of concern descended on me, reviving the same dread I'd felt while at K2. As I rode the elevator the awful events in woods with Vernon came back to haunt me.

I hadn't chosen the time or place; Vernon had . . . the trailhead at noon. I had tried to control the action, sneaking up on him . . . but he'd ambushed me. By the time the elevator reached the top floor, I decided I needed a plan so that next time Sniggy and his pals ganged up on me, I'd have the advantage.

I greeted Aunt Min, gave her an up-beat account of the day at school, and walked to my room with the comment: "Thought I'd write a note to Mom before dinner . . ."

"That's fine, Casey. She'll be glad to hear about how you helped solve our cannery problem."

I did write Mom a quick note, jotting down news about my getting on well at school, especially in Mr. Drake's science class. Then I lay back on my bed to plan and shape the clash I knew was coming.

twenty-six

BR'ER RABBIT AND THE BERRY PATCH

I had reasons to feel sorry for myself, but refused to think about being punched out, or my sore shoulder and my blurry eye. Instead, I propped a pillow behind me, said a short prayer for help, and began to develop a plan. Maybe I could even set a trap. How could I do that?

Of all things, I got to thinking about the Uncle Remus folktale of Br'er Rabbit being hunted by the fox. Maybe somehow the clever story might prompt a small miracle. I got an idea! I jumped up and got busy. I began by picking a small mirror out of the trash.

Down the street one block toward school, I'd noticed a ravine filled with blackberry vines. Because rabbits aren't hurt by briers, in the story of Br'er Rabbit, he fooled the fox by escaping into a brier patch. I thought of blackberry thickets, with vines known for their large thorns . . . actually a type of brier patch. If I could lure Sniggy's gang into the ravine, I might do more than simply pull a Br'er Rabbit escape. I wanted to settle the issue of intimidation.

With all this in mind, I began to piece together a plan of

action.

The next morning Sniggy's band of three elbowed their way down the hallway. Gene and I were heading to our next class. Pleased with the timing, I put the first part of my plan into action. Gene didn't seem to notice as I jockeyed the two of us just behind the band of three. I talked loud enough to be heard over the hubbub of student noise.

"Hey, Gene," I began. "On the way home, I noticed ripe blackberries down in the ravine. They're really good eating!"

"Yeah, but you have to be careful. The vines are full of nasty, sharp thorns."

I raised my voice. "Oh, a few thorns won't bother me. After school today I'm going to fill my lunch sack with berries to take home for breakfast."

Out of the corner of my eye, I caught a glimpse of Chisel. He turned his head just enough so that I could be sure he'd heard me. Now, would he and the others take the bait?

Through the day, whenever I had a spare minute, I reviewed my plan for the showdown. If the Sniggy gang wanted to get even with me for foiling their plan on the first day, they would think the ravine the perfect place.

I waded into my assignments; still, the morning classes dragged by and the afternoon seemed endless. I thought of Janet. Her pretty auburn hair and hazel eyes might well make the other girls a little envious of her. I admired Veronica, for reaching out to her, a new student, as Gene had with me. Thank God for friendly kids!

Such thoughts helped for a while, but my after-school plan soon re-surfaced. I knew it could work, but the gang had to bite. Everything depended on them following me down into the berry thicket.

At three o'clock, I left everything in my locker except my lunch bag, hoping that the gang wouldn't notice my traveling light. As I made an unhurried exit, I saw Sniggy talking with Mr. Drake outside the science room. It looked like Sniggy'd got hit with detention, which probably meant no confrontation in the ravine today. Drat! I'd really hoped to challenge the gang today. Oh well, I'd just have to try again another day.

As I walked glumly up the street, I approached the corner where I'd planned to climb down into the ravine that, I knew, served as a twenty-foot-deep drain ditch for the streets above. Blackberry vines seven feet high covered most of the lower area, including the part where rain runoff entered a culvert.

Yesterday I realized the need to see behind me without turning my head. With that in mind, I'd picked a small make-up case out of Aunt Min's trash to use as a rear-view mirror.

I'd almost given up being followed. Even so, I slowly raised the mirror to my eye, only to be shocked by the view. There, only a block behind, Chisel and Buddy ran with heads down. I could imagine being attacked and thrown into the brambles below.

With pounding heart, I stepped to the guard-rail and vaulted over to the edge of the ravine. If I could keep my nerve, my plan could still work with two bullies out of three.

I scrambled down the ravine's steep slope to the vines that grew out of the mud and grass at the bottom. Yesterday I'd been down there with a pair of clippers Aunt Min used to tend her house plants, and had cut a kind of tunnel. Now a canopy of thorny vines led into the thicket. I dropped to my knees and began to crawl toward the culvert at the other end. Low-hanging thorns caught my shirt. I stopped, released the vine, and moved on to the culvert, a cement pipe some thirty inches in diameter that extended under an apartment building. I left the thorny berry vines behind and crawled through the big pipe to the end, slipped out, and ran up to the street and around to the guard-rail at the edge of the ravine once more.

I arrived just as my two pursuers reached the bottom.

"Hey!" I yelled. "If it's a fight you're after, you'll have to come up here."

Chisel and Buddy, clearly confused, looked at each other for a second, then rushed to climb back up to street level. Since they'd seen me vault over the rail, I heard them muttering, "What's goin' on? How'd he get up there?"

Chisel came first. I timed my next move with precision. Just before he got to the top, I jumped over the rail, and hit him with what I had called, back in Brooklyn, my "jaw-breaker" punch.

Chisel fell to the bottom with his long frame arched back. He screamed in agony as a thick mass of berry vines broke his fall. Thrashing amid a thousand thorns, he screamed, "OW! ARRRAH! . . . BUDDY, DANG YOU! GET UP THERE! . . . SMASH HIM! BASH HIM GOOD!"

Buddy cautiously climbed up to me. As he gained footing at the top, I threw a feint, a round-house motion with my right that stopped just before impact.

Buddy, expecting to fend off the blow, raised his arm and leaned away. The pulled punch threw him off. He almost fell forward, then reared back again and teetered on the edge, arms wildly flailing in circles in an effort to regain his balance.

I couldn't resist. I let go with another jaw-breaker.

Buddy screamed as he fell. "OH NOOOO!"

Frantically trying to get out of the way, Chisel yelled: "NOOO!" Then, "ARUGHH! OW! OW! YOU IDIOT!" as Buddy smashed into him, cracking ribs and forcing thorns into Chisel's back. The two were a mass of intertwined arms, legs and thorny vines – covered with puncture wounds, scratches and mashed berries. Then the two began to fight each other in a wild, frustrated frenzy.

The yelling and screaming aroused the neighborhood.

Windows flew open and passers-by rushed over to peer down at the writhing boys.

I sauntered over to a woman who'd leaned out of her window, craning to see the cause of the commotion.

"Excuse me, ma'am," I yelled. "It sounds like one young man is causing the other a great deal of pain. Might you have a telephone?"

"Yes, yes I do. Should I call the police?"

"Yes, ma'am, it would be well to do that. Ask them to hurry."

Five minutes later, having left Chisel and Buddy in the good hands of concerned citizens with police on the way, I stood at the washtub in the basement of our apartment. I'd changed into clothes I'd concealed behind the stairwell. After rinsing mud and stains from my school clothes, I hung them up to dry.

Only a few minutes later than usual, I walked into the apartment and greeted Aunt Min. As I strolled down the hall to my room, the grandfather clock read, 3:45. The skirmish had taken less than an hour. Feeling at ease with myself, I leaned back on my bed and opened a letter from my mom.

Dear Casey,

Your latest letter gave me great comfort. It's reassuring to know that you've done well in the care of your Uncle Harry and Aunt Louise. I have fond memories of growing up in our pleasant home, Overton Manor. Harry, Minnie and I must have had many of the same experiences as your three cousins have now; enjoying the gardens, the beautiful grounds and, of course, the indoor swimming pool.

When you described the activities at K2 Ranch, they revived similar memories. I also loved to ride the horses there, and had several to choose from. The two farm dogs at that time often went along and chased rabbits as I rode along Funnel Creek.

I think it very nice that you have decided to pay a visit to your Aunt Minnie and Uncle Carl in Seattle. I've sent them a note of thanks.

Casey, I first met your father shortly after my high school graduation. As I prepared to leave for my first year of college, one night my father, Chester, invited Sgt. Dan Jones home for dinner. Your father-to-be had just purchased two hundred head of K2 beef cattle for the army. After a short courtship, Sgt. Dan and I decided to get married.

My family didn't approve, so we eloped and lived at Fort Monmouth in New Jersey. When your father got out of the army, he landed a job at the foundry and we moved to Brooklyn.

When my father, Chester Kinsman, died I inherited part of the K2 Ranch. Now your Uncle Harry and Aunt Louise have asked me to come back to Arborville. How would you like to live there with me, Casey? Write me a letter soon. I'd like to know your thoughts about joining our family, Kinsman clan, in Arborville.

As always with love,

Your Mom

I sat reflecting on our family history, then felt a pang of sorrow. "Oh Mom!" I thought. "You must have thought I decided on the spur of the moment to make the trip to Seattle. I should have written about the difficult times in my letters. I spared you the awful details. You don't know about Vernon trying to get rid of me."

Talk about mixed feelings! I couldn't concentrate on this new idea of Mom coming out and me going back to live at K2 just now.

At that moment the doorbell rang, and interrupted my thoughts.

I strolled out as Aunt Min opened the door. There stood two policemen.

"Excuse me, Ma'am," began one. "Is there a boy here named Casey?"

I stepped forward: "I'm Casey. How can I help?"

"Well, we heard from two young hooligans that just got themselves into a fracas down the way, that a classmate of theirs . . . you . . . started the whole thing."

"Why, that's hardly believable," said Aunt Min. "Casey here is my nephew and not the kind of boy who is prone to rowdiness." Aunt Min drew herself up tall. "Besides, he's been here at home for the past hour."

The second policeman looked me over closely. "Yes, ma'am. But did you actually see Casey here enter the apartment when he came home?"

"Yes, I did."

"Was he wearing the same clothes as now?"

"The same," Aunt Min answered.

I spoke up: "Thanks, Aunt Min, but I should tell what I know about this."

The officers brightened up.

"Because I'm new in school, Perry and Buddy talked about initiating me. They followed me on my way home from school and jumped me at the ravine down the block. I slipped over the rail. Perry came after me, lost his balance and fell into the vines below. Buddy came on right away and he fell too."

"Well, son," said the first officer, "your clothes don't show any signs of having been down in the ravine, so I tend to believe your story. Also we've had trouble with these two before. They'll have some explaining to do about being in your neighborhood. They live in the opposite direction from school."

"Do you want to file charges for being attacked?" asked the second officer.

"No officer, as you can see, I'm unhurt."

I smiled inwardly and gave a sigh of relief as the police

left.

At dinner, I related some of Sniggy's exploits with Perry and Buddy. "On the first day, I got the squeeze play in the hallway. Aside from a few threats, nothing more happened until this afternoon."

Uncle Carl looked concerned. "I didn't know about some of the boys threatening you, Casey."

"Well," said Aunt Min, "let's hope the incident today discouraged them."

Ready to change the subject, I asked, "Have we heard from Uncle Harry?"

"Yes, Casey. He's been delayed again. This time indefinitely. He asked me to return his suitcase to Arborville."

Uncle Carl went on. "As things stand, with you still under Dr. Kraft's care, and just starting a new school term, well . . . your Aunt Minnie and I hoped that you would be staying on here with us . . . at least until the end of the semester in December."

Certain that Mom wouldn't be moving out west quickly, I replied, "That would suit me fine." Then I added, "It's good of you to have me."

The next morning, Gene and Veronica stood waiting for me at the school-yard gate. Gene began excitedly. "Casey, we heard that Chisel and Buddy got hurt falling into that ravine . . . where you were going to pick berries."

Veronica's eyes narrowed as she lowered her voice dramatically. "We think you planned the whole thing. It's too much of a coincidence! The gang of three threatened you and then soon after those two are limping around with scratches all over them."

With raised eyebrows I tried to manage an innocent look.

"Limping? Scratches? What would I know about that?"

Gene nudged me as we walked to the entrance. "O.K., guy. We understand. Best not to talk about it, right? Not even with us."

Gene's wisdom proved out as we entered the main hallway and Sniggy came into view, sauntering toward us with a casual air about him. We kept talking and knew better than to stare as he passed by. As far as I could tell, Sniggy hadn't even glanced our way.

Gene gave me an elbow. "Get that! Trying to be the really cool customer, acting like nothing at all happened to his buddies."

"Well, yes, on the outside, but inside he's gotta be seething and snorting fire. Since the police were in on it yesterday, Sniggy wouldn't say or do anything in the open."

Veronica asked, "So you don't think it's over?"

"I think it's over with Chisel and Buddy, but Sniggy's still out to get me somehow."

twenty-seven

PUSHING MY LUCK

After the showdown, I settled into school. Classes and activities filled days that stretched into weeks. Two or three days a week I joined my new friends to talk things over after school, and on Saturday we rode the trolley downtown for a movie followed by ice cream sodas. I could afford the treats because Uncle Carl gave me a regular allowance. When I thanked him, he would always thank me in return for my helping to save his cannery business.

Janet liked to chat, and I'd never known anyone quite so interesting. Sometimes she told me about her older brother, recently out of the army and looking for a job. She got a laugh from us with her hilarious description of teaching her little sister how to milk a cow back in North Dakota. She taught me to like ice cream sodas and milkshakes. I discovered creamy pineapple shakes to be the most delicious thing I'd ever tasted.

One beautiful Saturday, as the four of us wandered a waterfront street, we noticed a small restaurant. I was amazed at the entrance, decorated with fish-nets, anchors and several seashells oysters with mother of pearl, blue mussels and scallops. But Veronica noticed a curiosity shop next door. "Before lunch, let's see the Alaska Gold Rush curios on display in here. I've heard they're fascinating."

Fascinating they were. Gene knew about the Gold Rush from school, but mostly from his grandfather, who had traveled north from this Seattle waterfront in 1898, in hopes of striking it rich.

Among all the artifacts, miner's picks, shovels and pans, Gene pointed out a big wind-up music box. "Look," he said excitedly. "It says this is from one of those saloons in Skagway." He wound it up, and a two-foot metal disk with fingers on it began to turn under a series of musical prongs and fill the air with lively music.

Never had we seen so many relics of an historic event. Hundreds of photos lined the walls, depicting men and women who had been among the thousands who had swarmed to Alaska in search of gold.

Gene stood before a picture of a steamboat. "Look! This is when the big news of gold up north hit here. It says, 'In July of 1897, the steamer Portland landed here with a ton and a half of gold on board.'"

"Skidoo! That must have been exciting."

"Yes, my grandfather said that in 1893 a financial panic hit the country. Seattle had been growing on the wealth of lumber and fishing. Mostly young men had built Seattle with the help some young women too, like the Mercer Girls, who'd traveled here from New England. But these pioneers were middle-aged during the really tough early 1890s. Then the gold fever hit and the whole area, Portland, Tacoma, Seattle and Vancouver, B.C., too, all began to prosper."

Veronica added, "Yes, in history class, I learned that few of those who risked everything they had in hopes of finding gold, actually struck it rich. Many died of cold and disease. Others came back broken in health and penniless."

I got a sick feeling in my stomach as I looked at the gaunt faces of those in the pictures. Most of them looked lost and miserable. "The lesson of history here is clear. Those who stayed in Seattle and sold supplies, did well... and most of those who went north didn't."

Then I reflected on my own relocation. I missed my mom, my dad, Mr. Lambrusco, and the friends I'd left behind in Brooklyn. Then at times, I thought of the wonderful Kinsman clan and I got a tight feeling of longing for all of them. When I began to dwell on my happy, energetic cousins, the urge to rush down to the train depot and travel back to them would have been overpowering if I hadn't forced myself to push them out of my mind.

Still, the stimulating fresh air, the busy city streets, Gene, Veronica and Janet, made for a pleasant life in this bustling city. My eye was back to normal, and Dr. Kraft didn't need to see me again for a year. My shoulder felt good, and the small scars on my face were the only reminder of that bad day in the woods.

I'd discovered an old barbell in the basement and began lifting it for several minutes a day. After a month of working out, not only had my shoulder returned to normal, the muscles of my upper body bulked up in size and strength. Maybe the milkshakes helped too.

I'd remembered Aunt Minnie had mentioned in her letter that I might help out in the seafood business. So one day Uncle Carl agreed to give me a job on Saturdays. I worked in the cannery warehouse, where thousands of cans of salmon were labeled and put in cardboard cases that I helped stack high around the walls. I filled orders too, lifting the cases onto conveyors where they rolled out to waiting boxcars or trucks.

Walking the sidewalks up the many hills helped build up my

leg muscles. By November, I reached a state of health and physical well-being I'd never known before. In my letters to Mom, I didn't mention this change in me. She would soon move to K2. I planned to return to Arborville just before Christmas. I recalled the day before I got on the train last August, when I'd needed Uncle Harry and Neva to help me walk. Lately I'd imagined getting off the train and having a joyful reunion with Mom and the others. I wanted my new, healthy physique to be a surprise for everybody.

These thoughts gave me a thrill of happy anticipation and prompted me to throw the heavy cases of canned fish on the stack with such vigor that the warehouse foreman asked me to add three days a week after school to my work schedule.

I especially loved anticipating Christmas at Overton Manor. I just knew the Kinsman clan would have a big beautiful tree and lots of wonderful presents. From out of the kitchen, Sally and Aunt Louise would produce fine pastries and delicious holiday food of all kinds. And how we'd sing carols! Neva and I might even work up some special holiday numbers for piano and guitar.

These thoughts reminded me to do some early shopping. From my cannery earnings, I bought a nice fountain pen for Uncle Harry, a lace handkerchief for Aunt Louise, a silk scarf each for Annie and Colette, and a small music box for Neva that played "On the Wings of Song." For my mom I found a beautiful cameo pin.

Near the end of the season, the cannery ran two full shifts, so Uncle Carl spent long hours on the job. One morning at breakfast, Aunt Min brought up my idea of selling salmon waste for fertilizer.

"Your Uncle has been so busy lately, he hasn't had a chance to talk to you about the new addition he's working on."

"New addition?"

"Yes. My brother Harry likes the idea of drying the fish waste from the cannery, packaging it up and selling it for fertilizer . . . your idea, I think."

I almost jumped out of my chair.

"Yes, I thought at first it might be useful for the barley we raise on K2, but since then, I've heard about all the lettuce, celery and cabbage they raise out in the valley south of here, and I think maybe the produce farmers might use it there."

"Right again, Casey. Don Clodell came up with another part of the operation. At his suggestion, we'll not only dry the salmon waste in our new addition, but in a separate, smaller dryer, we'll produce top-quality alder-smoked salmon."

"Umm, that sounds delicious."

"It is. It's delicious. We expect to sell it through delicatessens and specialty food shops."

"Aunt Min, I'm curious. Is Harry Kinsman investing in the fertilizer and smoked salmon business?"

"Yes, Casey. He's asked around and thinks there is a market for our new products."

With all the activity, thoughts of Red Snapper Dunn, the crew of the Silver Belle, and Sniggy seldom crossed my mind. Then, one Sunday afternoon, Gene came over to the apartment, and we took time off from studying for a literature exam for a few cookies. As a surprise treat, aunt Min poured us each a glass of cola. We enjoyed its sweet, unusual flavor.

"Casey, I think you need to be on your guard," Gene began. "Veronica overheard some of the guys talking about a few of the fishing boats getting ready to leave for Alaska."

"What's that got to do with me?"

"Press gangs. If a boat captain is short a crew member or two, he'll send out some of his crew to kidnap men, bring them back and press them into service on the long haul up to Alaska."

"I've heard of that. Its called being shanghaied."

"Yes, and some of that is going on right now down on the waterfront."

"Do you think Red Snapper Dunn might send out a press gang?"

"Yes, and although they usually pick up their men at the waterfront bars, I think they might actually target you."

The idea of being kidnapped on board a boat to Alaska gave me a jolt.

"Thanks for the warning, Gene, I'll be looking over my shoulder."

Actually, I realized it made sense for Captain Dunn to force me to join his crew. I'd grown so strong and healthy that I'd probably make a good deck hand. Then too, the Snapper held a grudge against me and wanted to get even.

The following Wednesday, a normal school day, I finished my warehouse shift at nine o'clock in the evening. Near exhaustion, I hurried to the corner and waited for the trolley to take me up the hill.

The glow from the surrounding buildings helped to light up the street. I turned, noticed that fog was rolling in, and peered back down the street. The hair on my neck stood up as three large men silently made their way toward me.

"A press gang!" I thought. With a surge of energy, I sprinted away up the street. Bone-weary after four hours of heavy lifting in the warehouse, I sought refuge through the open door of The Anchor. A stale smell hit me. In this waterfront tavern, prohibition wasn't being enforced. At the bar, twenty or thirty men sat with mugs in front of them. No one paid any attention to me as I walked to the back, except a young man on the last stool. I stopped, stared and recognized him. He looked at me and wrinkled his brow. I stood silently as we both tried to remember where we'd met before..

Then it hit me. "Benny, Benny from the Bronx."

Benny wrinkled his forehead even more and put out his hand. "Yes, but I'm trying to place you. Were you at Volunteer Park for the Labor Day picnic?"

"No, we met on the train after Chicago."

A big smile erased Benny's wrinkles. "Oh yeah! Now I remember. You're the boy who got off at some little town and never got on again. The conductor grabbed your bag and threw it off."

"Yes, I guess I've changed some since that day."

"You sure have. Now you're a man."

"Benny, I'm in trouble. I think a press gang's after me."

"What! My God! Quick, take the door to left. It leads to the alley. I'll tell 'em you're in the men's room."

In seconds I'd burst out into the alley, past a jolly couple singing "The Bowry," and jumped on the trolley a minute later.

Had it been a close call? Or had I been "spooked" by Gene's warning of being kidnapped? By the time I stepped down to the curb near the apartment, I felt foolish. I'd overreacted. In the foggy darkness, my weary mind had triggered panic.

Oh well. No harm done. After the usual shower, some milk, and a prayer, I settled in for a welcome night's sleep. I whispered my last thought of the day, "Benny from the Bronx . . . what a coincidence . . ."

CAPTAIN DUNN

twenty-eight

AUNT MIN SETS MY MIND ABUZZ

As the season drew to a close, most of the workers no longer worked the cannery's lines and retorts. The main floor fell silent. Office and warehouse workers stayed on. I could have continued my part-time position, but now I felt that I needed to give my job to someone who really needed it.

Now I had more time to devote to studying, having fun with Gene and the girls, and reading. I considered turning out for football, but the team had been practicing for six weeks already and I would have been a rookie. Besides it hadn't been all that long since I'd healed up.

I really hit it off with the librarian. She recommended one excellent book after another. During these late fall days, I always had two or three interesting books around. I read <u>Treasure Island</u>, by Robert Louis Stevenson. When I finished it, I went on to his <u>Kidnapped</u>.

This was a truly fine time in my life. I loved living with my kind aunt and uncle. Once after breakfast, Aunt Min sat enjoying the view out our living room window as she looked up from the bright threads of a needlepoint project.

I put down <u>Kidnapped</u> to feast my eyes on the panorama of snowy mountains. When I rejoined the Kinsman family, I'd miss Seattle with its beautiful scenery and my family and friends here. On an impulse, I asked a few questions about the family background.

My questions and Aunt Min's answers ranged from the early days of grandpa Wil, to her father, Chester, and on to the present with Uncle Harry. Aunt Louise, the present woman of the house at Overton Manor, carried on a tradition of fine Kinsman ladies. Now there were three young ladies growing up in that tradition.

I encouraged Aunt Min to talk first about Annie, then Colette and lastly Neva. Aunt Minnie stated that the cousins displayed few personal shortcomings and all three were blessed with fine personalities and not only likable but downright lovable dispositions.

As she made this last observation, Aunt Min put down her sewing and looked at me with a faint smile. "You haven't known them long, Casey, but can you say the same?"

"What?" I stammered. "Do I think they're lovable?"

Aunt Min went back to her needlepoint. "I suppose you're going to tell me that your feelings for them are only as a brother for his sisters."

"Yes. That's exactly it," I declared. "It's the way it should be with cousins. I have absolutely no other feelings for any of them."

Aunt Min cocked her head slightly. "Well, to quote Shakespeare: 'Methinks he doth protest too much.'"

I'm sure my face turned red. "Aunt Min! How can you say that!"

"Well, Casey. I'm sure you'll do what's right in the months and years ahead. I've come to know you as a truly fine young man of excellent character."

"You're telling me this so that I'll be on my guard and best behavior, aren't you?"

"Yes, of course."

"Well, then we can change the subject. I wanted to ask if there would be times when I could come back to visit. I have friends here now, and I've been really happy with you and Uncle Carl."

Now Aunt Min looked at me with great kindness. "Oh, Casey. You must know how much we love you. Promise to return often . . . maybe spend a good part of your summers here . . . the weather then is quite exceptional . . . maybe your mother would visit too."

"I will, I promise."

Aunt Min casually continued her sewing. "However, Casey . . . before we leave the subject of the Kinsman girls, I need to say one more thing. Though all are loved deeply, and with no distinction . . . one is adopted."

Toward the end of the conversation, I had begun to feel secure in my own mind; now this revelation left me speechless; my thoughts began to whirl.

twenty-nine

LEAVING ON A BAD NOTE

Rain pelted down. From the apartment window I could barely see across the street. Once or twice it had rained like this in Brooklyn, but I'd forgotten how it could change my view of things. At school, I'd really enjoyed watching the first two football games, with Gene and the girls. We sat in the stands, sang with the band, and ate popcorn on sunny afternoons. But umbrellas didn't work well while sitting down, and football played in a torrent was different. Once, when our running-back was tackled, he slid for two more yards. This is what my principal back in Brooklyn meant when he said Seattle has a "maritime climate." Hey! That means rain!

For a week it rained without a single sun break. The Duwamish River, near flood stage, caused some folks to move. The ravine in our neighborhood served its purpose. Water gushing from every place funneled down through the blackberries and filled the culvert where I'd crawled to safety with Chisel and Bud behind me.

During a glum Friday afternoon I got the urge to visit the warehouse at the cannery again. It had been over a week since

I'd left my part-time job, and I thought it would pass some time to see how the shipments of salmon were going.

As I traveled to the waterfront on the trolley, a pleasant thought hit me.

"Skidoo! Today's pay-day! Another good reason to visit the cannery."

I began to calculate my earnings. A ball-park figure would be about $50. I'd never earned that much money in my whole life. Benny had called me a man when I'd seen him that night at The Anchor. Yes! I felt like a man. I felt a surge of pride and took a deep breath as I jumped off the trolley and ran to the cannery gate.

Inside, I wandered around the warehouse, greeting the fellas on the job before entering the office. Mr. Clodell was at the counter.

"Hello, there, Casey. It's certainly good to see you again. How have you been?"

"I've been just great." I smiled.

"Well now, I'll get you your pay. I see here that you have 52 dollars and 50 cents coming. For part time employees, we pay in cash."

I blinked in appreciation as Gene's dad counted out the green bills, put them and a fifty-cent piece in a company envelope, and handed it to me.

We chatted for a few minutes, then I left the office. On my way out, I saw a white envelope tacked to the door with CASEY JONES written on it.

Inside I read:

Casey,
I heard you were here. Please meet me at the weigh-in dock.
I want to show you an interesting follow-up to your discovery of how the weight

of the fish had been rigged.
Uncle Carl

Eager to re-visit the place where Gene and I had solved the mystery, I ran down the steps and across the side of the deserted main floor, and stood under the cover for the conveyor platform. I focused on the scale area trying to see though the rain.

"Uncle Carl!" I shouted.

No answer.

"He's gone." I thought, "I shouldn't have talked so long with Mr. Clodell."

Suddenly everything went black. I struggled, but I was no match for the heavy arms and hands that bound me tight. I could feel rough canvas on my face.

Covered with a tarpaulin, then knocked off my feet, I sensed being carried across the dock, then lowered head-first down a hatch. My muffled yells and kicking didn't bother my attackers who quickly dropped me on a hard floor below decks.

"Untie him!" came the order.

As the ropes that bound me were loosened, I realized I'd been abducted aboard a fishing boat.

To my horror and dismay, just as the canvas came off, I heard another order: "Cast off fore and aft. Take her out!"

I sat up in the hold of a boat dimly lit by a whale oil lamp. Across from me sat none other than Bin Dunn, also known as Red Snapper, the captain of the Silver Belle.

For a full minute, he just sat there chuckling, as my fear of him grew. He wasn't smiling. It was a mirthless laugh.

Finally, he just glared, seemingly enjoying the moment. "Well, well, Mr. Jones, might you be any relation to the Jones of Davey Jones' Locker?"

For once, I'd not been asked about the rail-roader. Instead, Snapper gave the question about my name a nautical twist.

Before I could find my voice, I found out how Captain Dunn acquired his nickname, "Snapper." He suddenly reared up and gave me a stinging snap with a large leather strap. The blow found its mark on my still sensitive left shoulder. The intense pain gave me a flashback to Vernon.

"Answer me!" he roared, and raised his arm for another snap of the strap.

"NO!" I yelled. "I don't know Davey Jones."

This time, smiling as he laughed, Snapper sat down and leaned so close I could smell his foul breath. "You cost me money with your nosing around at the scale. Now I'm going to get it back. Fer starters, let's have that nifty pay envelope I saw Mr. Clodell give you in the office.

"Aha! I saw you through my spy-glass. We caught sight of you up in the office looking down, checking on the scale with that telescope. Well . . .that works both ways, hand over that pay!"

I quickly grabbed the envelope with a month's pay in it and emptied the cash into Captain Dunn's hand. As he counted the bills, I thought of making a run for it before we got too far from the dock to swim back.

Then Snapper rose to his feet to go, but first he reached down and securely fastened a leg iron on my ankle. Now chained to the deck, I'd lost any chance to escape.

"This fifty is a down payment for what you owe. I'll work the rest out of you."

With another coarse chuckle, he gave me a parting shot, "The crew said tacking that phony note to the door wouldn't work. They said you were too smart to take the bait. HA! They were wrong. Ol' Snapper's smarter than all of you."

SNAP. "TAKE THAT! for finding the fish hooks in the cart, AND THAT!" SNAP, "for finding the magnet."

I'd turned to receive the two stinging hits on my back.

As he left, the captain picked up the lamp, leaving me in the dark as the Silver Belle's steam pistons picked up their powerful rhythm.

thirty

A NIGHT OF TORMENT

Lying there below decks, heartsick and despondent, I shuddered from the cold and the damp.

As we left the shelter of the bay, heading out into the channel, the boat lurched from side to side. Then the rainstorm intensified the rocking motion. Thrown against a bulkhead I cried out, "OWW . . . UGHH!" but stifled other outbursts for fear that the captain would hear and return with his strap. Powerless to resist, I continued to roll on the foul-smelling planks.

I struggled to sit up. With my back to the bulkhead, I braced my feet against the cleat that held my chain and avoided the battering blows to my body. But I couldn't hold the position. My legs cramped up on me and I had to lie down. Again the restless sea took command of me. After a few minutes my muscles felt the fatigue from resisting the relentless rolling.

I endured the torturous torment until I sensed the boat taking a new tack. The rocking motion changed to a slower, fore-and-aft pitching as we came around and headed into the waves. This caused me to slide back and forth, so I moved away from the bulkhead until the chain stretched tight and I could reach the bottom rung of a ladder. I stopped sliding but my moment of relief didn't last.

I cried out in despair as a wave of seasickness welled up. "Oh my God! I brought this disaster on myself. Like a stupid fool, I'd taken Snapper's bait!"

In a couple of weeks I'd have been with my mom . . . set to celebrate the holidays in the loving embrace of my new found Kinsman family. And here I am a prisoner and throwing up.

I prayed, "Oh God, help me!" as time and again my stomach rebelled against the sea's motion. The thought of spending an endless night rolling in my vomit wore me down.

I fell into a semi-conscious state of exhaustion as the squall ran its course and the waters finally calmed down. When I awoke, I noted with relief, the lack of pitch and roll. My hands had slipped from the rung. Now on my back, with my dry mouth wide open, I sensed someone in the hold with me. A voice came from out of the darkness.

"Casey, are you there?

I tried to answer, "Yes." When that failed, I rattled my chain in reply.

The person in the dark struck a match, lit a lantern, set it on the floor and squatted beside it.

I strained to see who had come to me. I knew it wasn't the captain.

The person spoke again. "While you're gettin' your bearings, I'll fill you in. The captain's laid in a course for Ketchikan. We'll be sailing what's known as the Inside Passage to Alaska."

The voice was familiar. As my eyes adjusted to the faint light, I realized with a start that Benny sat before me.

"Here's a jug of water," he said. "Let's begin to get your guts back to working with a few sips of this."

Benny had brought a bucket of fresh water and helped me

clean myself up some. He also gave me a wool sweater and a knit watch cap. My heart swelled with gratitude as I watched him coming with another bucket, this one with sea water, to mop up the mess I'd made. When he'd finished, he climbed the ladder, opened a hatch and emptied the bucket over the side. Cold salt air filled the hold from above. As I took a deep breath of it, my stomach began to match the calmness of the surrounding sea.

Benny set a bucket in the corner. "Now when you have to go, use this," he said. He took a blanket from under his arm.

"These are hard to come by. The crew knows we're headin' up a thousand miles into colder waters."

A blanket! Still hardly able to speak, I nodded my appreciation.

"The captain's expecting me topside, gotta turn to. Sorry I can't leave the lamp, but I'll be back soon as I can . . . maybe later you'll be up to eating some biscuits."

I dismissed the thought of food . . . still too soon, but I quickly rolled myself in the blanket that smelled of stale sweat, very thankful for the protection from the floor. My shoulders and elbows felt like I'd gone over Niagara Falls in a barrel.

So once again, left in complete darkness, I took another swallow of water and pondered my fate at the hands of the black-hearted Captain Dunn. At least now I had a friend on board.

thirty-one

BENNY'S BAD NEWS

BENNY

Strange that Benny should turn up, first in the bar and now here. I remembered him saying when we met on the train that he was heading west to take a job on a fishing boat. It had sounded so adventuresome. I had fancied myself poised on the deck of such a boat, catching fish with an admiring captain looking on. Such foolish fantasy!

I made myself think of fragrant early mornings at K2, riding out as rays of gold hit the forested hillside.

Only half awake now, I could almost feel Jasper's steady gait and I moved to match his rhythm. What a horse! We truly belonged together as I hurried him up the trail in the early light of day. I breathed in the pine-scented air. As we entered Cal's beautiful, woodsy hideaway I jumped off, eager to greet Lobo.

Lobo! He wagged his tail and bounded over to meet me. We, too, belonged together. I put my arms around his neck as he licked my cheek. Tossing a rawhide ball Cal had made for him, I cavorted with Lobo, who ran to retrieve it and then playfully avoided my rush to catch him. My brain avoided a return to the reality of my dark dungeon as warm, carefree thoughts rolled on.

Someone on the ladder! "Let it be Benny," I prayed and squinted in the lantern's light.

"How you doin' now?" asked Benny cheerfully as he set a tin plate before me. "That cranky stomach of yours gonna want some biscuits and bacon?"

I slowly chewed the biscuits, swallowing each bite with a swig of water. I wrapped the bacon in my handkerchief and put it back in my pocket for later.

Solid food helped to restore my voice. "Benny, you're a true Godsend. Thanks for helping me."

"I'm pleased to see you through your first day on board. It's more than I got when they chained me up down here, but then, we were still in port and I didn't get seasick."

"Benny! They shanghaied you, too?"

"The same night the press gang came into The Anchor, looking for you, they took me."

"No! What lousy luck!"

Benny wrinkled his brow. "No better than yours, I'd say," he replied with a half smile.

"So we're in this together. We'll work our way, fishing in Alaska?"

Benny shook his head. "You and I, Casey, we're set to work the halibut season, but . . . pardon the expression, you are in 'one fine kettle of fish.'"

"Why? Because I foiled the rigged scale set up?"

"Yes, and because you're the cannery owner's nephew, they may even hold you for ransom."

"Ransom! My God, not that!"

"We'd have left port several days ago, but the captain didn't want to head north without you."

"Snapper'd been waiting for me? Waiting for me to come to the dock so he could spring his trap?

"Yes."

I thought to myself, "and I'd just been thinking of myself, I'm a man, because I'd built up a few muscles. How stupid could one dumb kid be!"

Benny went on, and what he said next made the gloom in the hold even darker.

"The crew'd been grousing about wasting time in port. With the salmon season over, they were restless to head north. It was all Snapper could do to hold 'em off," Benny said.

"If I'd waited another day or two . . . stayed clear of the waterfront, I'd not be here in this mess."

"Right. Along with the fact that a kid from school met with the captain and encouraged him to wait. "Friday's payday," I heard him say. "Casey'll come down to pick up his pay."

"What! Sniggy met with Captain Dunn?"

"Yeah, and he even forged the note from your uncle."

In a fit of fury, I bumped back against the bulkhead, beating my head in frustration. Sniggy'd got his revenge!

Benny waited patiently for me to calm down. Then he offered advice: "You've had a spate of bad luck, don't let it eat at you. I think folks can make their own luck too. You and I need to make the best of it now and watch for a break."

I gave Benny a straight look. He deserved a good reply.

"That's the best advice I've ever heard. Thanks again, Benny. But when do I get this chain off?"

"I'd guess tomorrow, after we leave Bellingham. The captain wouldn't want you to jump ship while we're takin' on a load of coal."

thirty-two

DARK DAYS, BLACK NIGHTS

About mid-day we pulled into a Bellingham Bay coal dock. I put my hands over my ears to block the roar of the coal filling the aft hold. Then, fine coal dust sifted into my area and settled over me. Earlier, I'd eaten the bacon from my handkerchief, which now served as a filter for my nose and mouth.

An hour or so later, Silver Belle's engine throbbed to life and we were under way once again. Now maybe the captain would come for me. I folded the blanket and tucked it behind the bucket for safekeeping.

Benny'd guessed right. Minutes later, Captain Dunn slipped down the ladder with his lantern. My heart sank when, with a demonic flourish, he unlimbered his strap.

"Wake up, ya lazy lubber!" he yelled and, with a full swing, landed the most painful blow yet. "High time ya started to earn your keep!" He leaned down and unlocked my chain, kicking my leg free of the shackle.

"Get up, ya lout! I just promoted you to stoker!"

I'd looked forward to getting up on deck for a breath of fresh air, but Snapper shoved and kicked me through two portals separating the lower compartments. Then he ran me up metal steps. We bent low on a catwalk over the coal bunker below, and scrambled down into the suffocating, steamy air of the engine room.

At the far end, two huge pistons puffed and chuffed. The shaft entered a gearbox, then extended through the aft bulkhead to the boat's propeller. An unlit lantern swayed from a hook above. The only source of light came from the boiler's blazing firebox.

As the captain spoke to a short, muscular man, I quickly pulled off my sweater and shirt.

"Pete, you can take a break. This here scrubby kid is now a stoker."

"Yo!" yelled Pete, dropping his shovel and looking me over. "Youngster, you look like a poor excuse fer this job!"

Wanting to prove him wrong, I rushed to pick up the shovel.

Snapper rewarded me for my eager start with a whack from his belt on my bare back. "Avast there, ya lubber, til Pete lays in yer stoker duties!"

Smarting from the latest hit, I watched as Pete pointed to a steam gauge that read 190.

"Ye see this black hand, Lubber? It's pointing to 190. If it falls below 160 pounds o' pressure per square inch, yer head o' steam'll be too low to push the pistons. But if the hand gets up to 280, the boiler will blow the safety valve . . . unless it's stuck, then the whole boiler'll blow and we'd all wind up on the bottom o' the sea in Davey Jones' locker."

I noticed that since Pete had stopped shoveling coal, the hand had begun to drop.

Pete went on. "And Lubber, here's how to stoke a boiler."

Pete's face and bare chest, covered with coal dust, matched the color of his black, curly hair and bushy eyebrows. With deliberate ease, he ran the scoop shovel on the metal deck to the edge of the huge pile of coal. With a shump, the shovel slid in and filled; a lift, a smooth turn, a thrust, and several pounds of coal sailed into the waiting firebox directly under the boiler.

He grinned as he handed me the shovel. I imitated Pete's motion while he and the captain watched. I sensed that the captain would have snapped his strap again if I'd spilled a single piece of coal. Ten shovel-fulls later, the two left me to my new job.

After ten more shovel-fulls, I paused to catch my breath and check the steam pressure, only to get a worrisome 185 reading. Despite my best effort, steam pressure had dropped! With pounding heart I wiped the sweat from my eyes and pitched in again. I managed another ten, slower this time.

The seasickness had sapped my energy and I was gasping for air. I waited a full minute and noticed a jug of water hanging on a spigot near by. Sipping, so as not to overdo it, I swallowed twice and got my second wind.

Now I imagined the pressure dropping to 160. It seemed that I simply didn't have the energy to stoke this boiler by myself. I felt a welt on my back from the last snap from the strap. If the engines quit, I knew Snapper would come charging down here. He'd yell and beat me again. I continued shoveling and made myself count twenty more shovel-fulls before I collapsed on the iron deck.

I looked up at the gauge. It read 192!

Then I realized that with the engine running full, as coal entered the firebox, a delay of ten minutes or so occurred before the heat from it produced steam in excess of the pistons' demands. Pete must have been shoveling sparingly before I took over, which would account for the pressure drop.

I discovered a small stool and slumped down on it, staring in fascination as the needle on the steam gauge steadily rose to

196, then climbed five minutes later to 220, then continued on up to 260 with no sign of slowing.

Could it be that due to my inexperience, I'd blow the safety valve, filling the engine room with scalding steam? Or maybe even blow up the boiler!

With the pressure at 270 and still rising, I looked at the gauge closely. In the dim light, I noticed that the dial behind the needle had a danger zone colored red. It began at 275 pounds per square inch. Now the needle rose into the red, to 280.

I'd suffered from cold while chained in the forward hold. Now I poured sweat from the flaming heat of the firebox that glowed with streaks of cherry red. I staggered back and prayed that the pressure would stop rising. It did . . . after hovering at 282 for several minutes. Due to the high pressure, steam hissed from pipe fittings everywhere, but the safety valve held.

When the pressure slipped back to 270, my next concern was that the captain would slow or stop the engine. If that happened, I knew the pressure would shoot up again. But the boat chugged on, steadily pushing us farther north than I'd ever been before.

When the gauge showed 260, I closed the firebox door most of the way. It made sense to keep the heat inside. Enough light flared out for me to keep a check on that black needle.

I'd almost blown up the boat, and my mind was reeling.

As I rested on the stool leaning back on the bulkhead, I began a rough calculation of coal to steam pressure. My brain took over with a mind of its own, beginning with the engine's steady demand for steam, then to the effect on pressure of Pete's one shovel-full, plus my fifty.

Each shovel of coal had produced an approximate two-pound-per-square-inch rise in pressure within about ten minutes.

My mind then began to clock elapsed time by imagining

a sweep second hand of a stopwatch as I fed the firebox and checked the pressure gauge. I decided on 200 psi as the ideal pressure to maintain the boat's running speed. I added a minute hand to the mental second hand, and every five minutes I placed a lump of coal on the sideboard by my stool.

Five minutes went by before I decided to throw in another shovel-full, after which, the pressure continued to drop, but still read 242. After another five minutes, with a reading of 235, I added another shovel-full and noticed the pressure slide to 230.

I decided to add two shovel-fulls every five minutes until the pressure slowly dropped to 200 – and my breathing and heartbeat returned to normal. Now three shovels of coal every five minutes seemed right. I could handle that.

Perched on the stool, and with a sincere thanksgiving for answered prayers, I took a long drink of water.

Whew! For the first time in two days, I took stock of my new situation. My first thought: "Thank God I'm able to handle this stoker job!"

Keeping the steam up in the boiler is hard work, more than one stoker should be expected to do, but I seemed up to it and felt more like a man again.

Throughout these many weeks since I'd left New York, my thoughts had never been far from Mom, the home I'd left, and Dad.

Dad! My stomach cramped as my heart longed for him. He'd died on the job, shoveling coal!

Due to a strange turn of events, now . . . for the first time . . . I knew what Dad's job had been like.

My mood changed from sadness, to steely resolve. I'd make a go of this new life aboard Silver Belle out of respect for my dad! This line of work was good enough for him. It'll be good enough for me too. With faith and will, I'll put my best effort into it because I'm his son and a man now, too. I'll do it for that. And for that!

Three hours later, Benny came down with a smile and the usual furrowed brow. He brought my dinner . . . more biscuits and cold bacon.

"Casey," he began. "There are two bunks forward. You can use one of them."

Benny returned topside, after pointing out my new place to sleep. What an improvement over sleeping on the deck! The narrow, built-in bed had a thick mattress and a blanket. A rail ran the length of the open side to prevent one rolling out in rough weather. I assumed that Pete used the other bunk fastened to the opposite bulkhead.

Back in the boiler room, the biscuits and bacon released energy to my muscles that gave me energy to shovel the coal that in turn released the power to run the boat's steam engine. At Webster High, Mr. Drake would have appreciated the physics involved. I smiled at this concept of energy and motion. Yes, I'd wager that someone watching Silver Belle kick up its frothy wake, wouldn't guess that indirectly, biscuits and some smoked pork helped propel it.

thirty-three

SNAPPER STRIKES AGAIN

Another hour of constant concern for the correct pressure – I watched the level swing between 198 and 204, but considered this range all right. Then Pete returned and announced we'd each be working four-hour shifts around the clock on the long haul to Alaska.

Relieved of duty, I headed for my bunk with shirt and sweater in hand. Pete called after me, "Get back here at six bells." Six bells! I'd heard the bells, but hadn't understood that they were a shipboard way to tell time. Now I wouldn't have to use the lumps of coal to count the hours.

I needed rest and groped my way into the darkness forward. With my life now spent entirely below decks, I lost track of night and day. With no portholes, the only light came from the firebox or a lantern. I began to settle into a life lived below the waterline and at times in almost total darkness.

I felt my way past the bunk to retrieve the other blanket I'd left behind the bucket. The stoker's quarters were cold, but with two blankets, I slept warm and woke up after what I judged to be two or three hours . . . less than four anyway.

Just then, Benny entered with his lantern and sat on the

other bunk.

"Casey, you awake?"

"Yes."

"Brought you another meal. But first you gotta sign the paper."

"What paper? I asked.

"This paper that says, I swear that I am eighteen years old. Then, I hereby apply as able seaman on the Silver Belle for the duration of the fishing season. I agree to receive the pay of four dollars a week and my keep.

"The captain dated it as of two days ago when you came on board."

"But . . . but I'm not eighteen and I don't want to commit myself to working in the dark for weeks or months."

"Casey, you want Snapper to come down here with his strap?

"No!"

"If you don't sign this, he'll beat you until you do."

Dang! Snapper hadn't actually used his strap, but he'd struck again.

After I'd signed my name in the dim light, Benny took the paper and signed Ben Vanderhorn on a line under mine.

"Benny, why have you signed my application?"

"I witnessed your signature." Benny replied. "If the Coast Guard stops us and wants to take you off, the captain will show them this paper and I'll have to say I saw you sign it."

"But won't they realize I'm not 18?"

"You look 18 to me. Can you prove otherwise?"

"I don't have any identification at all, certainly none with my birth date on it."

"Eat your grub. You'll need it to do the work," Benny got up to go. "I'll leave the lantern and some matches. But light it for only a few minutes at a time."

I lay back stunned. The paper I'd just signed seemed to prevent my rescue. How depressing! I'd harbored thoughts of getting back to Seattle in the near future. Now, even if Uncle Carl should come after me, I'd be legally tied to this sea-going tub!

I had to escape. Escape! My only hope of getting my life back.

thirty-four

THE INSIDE PASSAGE

With my head in my hands, I smelled the aroma of something spicy from a dimly seen tray, and the delicious odor lifted my dejected mood. No more biscuits and bacon! On the sideboard stood a plate full of boiled potatoes covered with chile con carne. I savored every bit of it, and the coffee too from a large white mug . . . another hit. The stimulating liquid felt good all the way down. While warming my hands on the mug, I also enjoyed a thick slice of dark bread.

With a full stomach and warm inside and out, it occurred to me to wonder, "Why the good meal?" Probably the captain thought to keep me healthy enough to do the stoker's heavy work.

But what about Benny? Whose side did he really come down on? Lately he seemed to be doing the captain's bidding . . . even to forcing me to sign the false document and legalizing it himself. Was he truly on board against his will? On the train he'd claimed to have a job waiting.

I started up as I heard six bells and I scrambled aft. A minute later, Pete handed me the shovel and said, "We're comin' round into the wind. The bridge has called for extra steam.

You'll be busy."

Wind! I hadn't considered the effect of wind.

So far, there hadn't been much, or maybe even a tail wind. How much additional need for coal would a head wind demand? To prepare for the worst, I increased the rate of three shovelfulls every five minutes to four shovelfulls a minute. One shovelfull took me eight seconds to deliver. This allowed less than an eight second pause between each shovelfull.

Three steps in . . . shump . . . lift . . . turn, three steps forward, let fly, pause . . .

The new routine proved just right to power the boat into the wind. The pressure held steady at 210.

Three steps in . . . shump . . . lift . . . turn, three steps forward, let fly, pause . . . repeat.

The new and demanding rhythm of work continued without let up for half an hour. Fortunately, lifting cases of salmon back at the cannery had prepared me. A case of salmon weighed close to twenty five pounds. I'd fed cases on the warehouse conveyer for an hour at a time.

With the pressure reading 208, I paused for a water break. Breathing heavily, I was resting on the stool for a few minutes when Pete suddenly appeared. He seemed surprised to find me taking a break. He stared at the good pressure reading and raised his eyebrows.

"Looks like you can take a minute to learn about the speaking tube," he said.

I got up and followed him to the sideboard.

"Anytime we need to change speed, stop, or shift into reverse, it's done with this lever."

I noticed that the various speeds were clearly marked. The lever, now set next to FULL AHEAD, could also be set for HALF, SLOW, STOP and ASTERN.

Pete continued. "When the helmsman wants a change,

first he'll blow into the tube up there. That makes a whistle down here."

Pete picked up the end of the tube. "Then you'll listen to the direction by putting your ear to this end. Just remember, when you change from one speed to another, move the lever to stop first."

An hour later, when my aching muscles needed a rest, the pressure rose to 245. Back on the stool, I drank several swallows from the jug. The pulsating sound of the engine lulled my mind, my chin dropped on my chest and I dozed off.

At the shrill sound of a whistle, I awoke with a start, the stool slipped out and I sprawled on my back.

The speaking tube! It could be the captain!

As I raised the tube I heard, "Are ya there?"

I spoke into the tube, shouting above the roar of the engine. "Yes, yes, sir."

"Slow . . . cut speed to slow."

Again I answered, "yes sir."

I grabbed the lever with both hands and shifted it to STOP. As the engine quickly responded, I waited a second and pushed the lever back up to SLOW. With a piercing swoosh, steam again began to push the pistons, the shaft turned and Silver Belle moved ahead . . . but much more slowly.

I noticed Benny standing at my side. "The captain sent me down as a back-up, but no need, you did that just right."

"Why are we slowing down?"

"We're going to drop anchor at Powell Inlet. We need to run the channel up ahead in daylight."

Benny went on. "You're through for now. Pete will tend the boiler tonight so the fire won't go out, but once we stop, there'll be no need for steam 'til dawn tomorrow."

"Benny, I need a shower."

"No shower on board, but you can go over the side and

wash up."

Ten minutes later Benny handed me a bar of soap and a brush saying, "We're at anchor now. Come with me."

For three days I'd not seen daylight. When I jumped on deck I felt a thrill from my scalp to my toes. The chill, salt air tingled in my lungs and I shivered at suddenly being thrust into the open. Then, I stepped to the rail and drank in the most beautiful sunset I'd ever seen. I turned toward shore and my mind floated upward, dazzled by one of nature's best views: the grandeur of a dark green, thickly wooded hillside rising from the water's edge. From it, a large stream flowed into the bay.

On the Belle's aft transom, I ditched my clothes and splashed off as much coal dust as I could before lathering up with the brush. I then dropped into the bay to rinse off. The water, cold as ice, took my breath away. I climbed out shaking, picked up my clothes and clambered on up to Benny on the deck.

"No sense washing out your clothes, they'll be black again two minutes after you're back shoveling," he said. "Here, use this shirt to dry off and put it on with these overalls."

I accepted the clothes with thanks. Looking over Benny's shoulder while putting them on, I could see the crew's day-room area, a cabin just aft and below the wheel-house. Through the large portholes, I caught sight of three crewmen seated at table. "Probably having their evening meal." I thought.

Benny seemed to read my mind. "You're not going in there, Casey. It's back down below decks for you. I'll bring your meal . . . pork and beans tonight, I think."

"O.K., but I see someone about my age up near the bow. Can I take a minute to meet him?"

"No. That's Bruce. He's repairing nets. Maybe you can meet him at Prince Rupert, our next stop, but not now."

At hearing his name, the young man gave us a forlorn look.

Even at a distance, I could see how unhappily he returned to winding a heavy net piled in front of him onto a large wooden reel. From the look of him, he too had been brought on board against his will by the press crew. Pulling and tying nets all day would be as tedious as my stoker job . . . maybe even harder on the back.

I thought, "Poor Bruce. At sundown, he's still working instead of eating with the crew."

I stretched out on my bunk, refreshed after my bath in the bay, but uncomfortable in Benny's bib overalls and wool shirt. Still damp, I shivered in the dank hold. I longed to rub myself down with a nice, clean towel. It helped to put on the wool watch cap over my wet hair.

Bundled in blankets, I slipped into sleep, then roused up when Benny dropped off my meal.

"Hey, Casey, here's a nice surprise for you. Jube Setter, our first mate, caught some fish for our supper."

"Fish?" I replied sleepily.

"Yeh, ling cod . . . I like it better than salmon," Benny said as he turned to go.

I lit the lantern and pulled a chair up to the sideboard. A chunk of roast fish took up half the plate.

"Skidoo!" I said out loud as I noticed noodles and fried onions too. "What a meal!"

"Ummm," I rolled the tasty seafood around in my mouth. As I picked up the mug, I got another surprise; instead of coffee, I sensed something new; the aroma and taste of steaming hot tea with milk and sugar. "Simply delicious!"

Also new to me were some meaty chunks mixed with the onions. They tasted strange, I guessed: chopped cod liver. "Very nutritious!"

I was beginning to develop a respect for the cook.

thirty-five

MY EXPANDING WORLD

In the days that followed my brief adventure topside, I experienced a strange sense of self-satisfaction. I knew we traveled in what had to be the world's most beautiful waters. I simply couldn't pass through all this natural beauty with my view confined to the dreary black coal bunker illuminated by the orange glow from the boiler.

In my frustration, I decided to search the bulkhead above. I climbed the catwalk over the bunker, lantern in hand, and a thrill shot through me as I discovered a porthole covered with soot. I scrambled down to the boiler room locker and returned with soap and brush. As I wiped the glass with my sleeve, I blinked at the brilliant scene beyond.

The next three days passed magically. As the Belle steamed steadily up shimmering inlets, past a thousand tree-clad islets, I spent as much time as possible crouched on the catwalk, watching the wonders of my new world glide by. A captive, a slave of sorts, yet I now knew the delight of ancient mariners as they sailed these waters.

Other craft navigating these channels became part of my new adventure. While lying in my bunk, I'd noticed a sudden rise and fall as the Belle met a series of waves. I guessed that they came from passing water traffic. Now, from my porthole, I watched fishing boats, an ocean-going tugboat pulling a barge, and a true ship of the seas, a freighter with two smokestacks, steam past, each sending out its wake.

Also sailing north, a medium-sized passenger ship with a gold nameplate, Sitka Seafarer, overtook us. I could plainly see into its salon, where well-dressed men and women laughed and danced. At the rail one young woman, who reminded me of Colette, put her hand to her lips and, with a friendly gesture, blew a kiss to us as her sleek vessel gracefully glided ahead at twice our speed.

Inspired by her light-hearted greeting and glad for the girl and for the other happy people on board, I touched my grimy hand to my mouth and returned the warm salute.

As Pete began his shift, I sat on the stool and watched him work instead of tumbling into my bunk. He stoked with a truly smooth rhythm; no wasted motion. I tried to learn from him.

Then, as I peered at Pete silhouetted against the furnace's glare, I noted something that sucked the air from me in surprise. PETE WORE GLOVES!

I looked down at my hands, ugly and cracked. Much of the callus that had built up in my warehouse work had worn off, leaving new, raw skin underneath. Still, though swollen and stiff, I hadn't thought of my hands as I'd steeled myself to the job.

Just then, Pete paused and leaned on his shovel. "What in Hades you lookin' at?"

I slowly rose and took a step forward. "Pete, I need a pair of gloves."

Without hesitation, he handed over his to me. "Take these," he said.

"Thanks, but what about you?"

"I'll finish my shift without . . . got more in my locker. I wear out a pair a week."

I slipped into Pete's thick, leather gloves, still warm and sweaty; a good fit, with lots of wear left in them.

"I figure I owe you," I said.

"Naw, you don't owe me nothin'. Since you came on the job, I hain't never had it so good. Stokers gotta help each other. It's one life we live together down here, four hours at a chunk, and you've learned to shovel your share; you more than pull your weight."

Truly touched by this, I said, "Kinda like, what one puts down the other picks up."

"Yeh, you got it right kid. When you take good keer a ol' Belle's boiler, you're a layin' yourself out fer me too."

"I'll try to keep it up, but Pete . . . at our next stop, if you buy gloves, could you pick up another pair for me?"

"That I will, Casey me boy, but before we make our next port at Prince Rupert, we'll have to get past Ripple Rock."

"Is Ripple Rock a hazard?"

"It is, if you call almost a hundred vessels sunk or damaged, a hazard."

"Skidoo! What makes it so dangerous?"

"Well, it sits out there in Seymour Channel a stirrin' up a whirlpool, that's why. If we get caught in its current, like as not we'll be pulled right into the rock and the shoals around it."

Pete scowled: "It'd splinter our hull into match-sticks in less than a minute and we'd be up to our noses in sea water, with little chance to get out alive."

I got scared: "When will we be passing this Ripple Rock?"

"I figure in a couple of hours from now. Be back here by then, both of us need to be on duty. You can keep up good boiler pressure, and I'll handle the controls if the captain calls down orders."

I stumbled forward, gripped by the fear of drowning, or worse, being boiled like a lobster if the sea reached the firebox.

In danger of death, I fell asleep begging Heaven's help to see us safely by the menace in the channel. I dreamt that as we approached, the rock changed into a fire-breathing sea dragon that stood athwart the waterway, stirring up the waters with its long, spiny tail.

At four bells I awoke with a start and groped my way back to Pete, who seemed to be sweating more than usual.

"Take over," he said as he moved to the speaking tubes. "We gotta stay sharp now."

I built pressure up and turned to Pete. "I'm going to take a look out the port-hole."

"Make it snappy. We need ta keep up a good head of steam fer this passage."

Heart pounding, I climbed up, crouched and craned my neck. Would I get a look at the rock? Yes! Ripple Rock, like a huge black iceberg, emerged from a ghostly curtain of mist, and at that moment the Belle, caught in the dangerous whirlpool, shuddered and swerved hard to port, directly at the rock.

Wide-eyed, I watched in horror. The rock closed in as I heard the whistle and Pete excitedly confirming orders. I stayed glued to the porthole while the Belle vibrated into reverse and slowly came back around, barely avoiding disaster. Then, with our engines in full forward, we steamed so close to the jagged menace that dozens of seagulls on the rock took flight in alarm. One of the snow-white birds, wings flapping wildly, flew past my port hole and momentarily peered at me with one red eye.

Just then, another boat suddenly loomed ahead on a collision course with us. I glimpsed the man at the helm, spinning the wheel, frantically trying to miss both us and the rock as his fishing boat careened past, unable to avoid giving the rock a glancing blow.

Dashing back down to Pete, I described the events outside.

"Could ya tell how bad she was bashed?" he asked.

"No, right after the hit, I lost sight of her."

Pete rushed up topside and I went back to tending the boiler.

At sundown, we again put into a cove. Pete brought down my meal instead of Benny.

"You saw right," he said. "The captain says that boat was listing to starboard. He didn't see 'em dropping lifeboats, so they probably got the hole in her hull patched up."

"Patched up? How?"

Pete described how a crew has some loose timbers, batting and caulking material available for patching a small leak. After I'd finished eating, we went forward and he showed me how caulk, a mass of tar and canvas, could be jammed onto a gash in the hull and then braced with a timber.

Back in my bunk for four hours of sleep, thankfulness welled up. Our boat had avoided a collision . . . a dangerous brush with disaster in the whirling current at Ripple Rock. But the other fishing boat had not. I prayed that both the boat and crew would make it safely to port.

thirty-six

THE CAPTAIN'S GAMBLE

My early morning shift began with Pete squirting oil from a big can with a long spout on all the moving parts of the engine. In the meantime, I shoveled coal. As I finished the first set of five shovels, he came and stood near.

"Casey, the captain's about to take us through Chum Channel. He figures we can save half a day on the way up to Rupert."

I noticed Pete's face as the coal flared up. Frowning, he curled his lower lip like he'd bit into a quince. "I say it's a mistake. Ships of any size should steer clear of Chum Channel . . . rock cliffs drop straight down to water's edge. A flood tide in there could smash the Belle against a wall of rock and we'd all drown or freeze to death in icy waters."

When Pete took over, I rushed up to my porthole and stared at the wild country passing by. Pete hadn't stretched it. Rugged rocks on the shore gave way to sheer sandstone walls rising directly out of the sea. Peering ahead, cold fear returned as I noted the narrow route chosen by our brutal captain. I judged we were passing through the channel at low tide, because barnacles covered the wall of rock several feet up from the water's edge. I knew that when the tide turned, the current would be fierce in this narrow waterway. If forced against the wall, our wooden hulled boat could be smashed like a straw hut in a hurricane.

We ran the channel at top speed for maximum control. My heart pounded. As with Ripple Rock, we again sailed dangerous waters, skirting disaster. An hour dragged by as with every second I expected the Belle to careen against either one side or the other as we shot the gap. Full flood tide propelled us up straight stretches and around a bend. My cramped leg muscles protested, but I couldn't turn away as we ran the gantlet of this remote, northern sea-lane.

Another hour of passage, and I relaxed a bit. It seemed we might make it through after all. I needed rest before my shift began; I stretched out on my bunk. Minutes later, I awoke from a troubled sleep. The Belle was shuddering and shaking. Could it be that we'd come into conflicting currents caused by changing tides in this narrow channel?

Just then, the sharp crack of wood splintering against rock resounded through the hold. The worst had happened! The Belle, propelled by the roiling current, had suddenly swerved, sending her prow into the unforgiving channel wall.

Stumbling forward in the dark, I heard the sound of rushing water as I came to the point of the collision. Light from an open hatch above showed a parting of the hull's timbers, but thank God it appeared small enough to patch.

Clutching caulk with one hand, I balanced a wooden brace against my side. I aimed at the leak, and with an effort born of desperation, I rammed the mass of caulk into the rush of sea water that was fast filling the hold. I pushed the other end of the timber against the opposite bulkhead. It wedged tight; the leak had been stanched! Now with both hands I strained every muscle, heaving on the brace to secure it tightly as possible. The patch complete, icy water around my ankles still spurred me on until I felt Pete's hand on my shoulder.

"Avast, there! Back off! You got it as good as it can be for now."

Benny appeared out of the darkness and pried my hands from the brace. Heaving deep breaths and shaking with emotion, I pulled back. A shadow crossed in front of us. I looked up to see the captain peering down, inspecting the damage. He shouted down, "Good piece of work Benny . . . that's the kind of fast action I expect from the crew." Then he turned and called to the man at the wheel, "Steady as she goes at half speed. Resume course for Rupert."

Too shocked to speak, I realized that I'd stepped back into the darkness just before the Captain had looked down. He naturally thought it'd been Benny's fast work that had saved the Belle. As we sailed out of danger, I knew that I'd saved us all from disaster.

My shoveling shift dragged by. At half speed, I spent three or four minutes at a time on the stool, still keyed up by the close call. At one point, I sat up and said to myself, "Hey! This tub could be sitting on the bottom right now. What's the expression? Davey Jones' Locker? We'd be there if I hadn't patched up that gash in the side. You'd think someone would have given me a little show of thanks."

I wondered if Benny would set the captain straight . . . tell him that I deserved full credit for my quick work. Probably not. Oh well, I'm still alive, and that's reward enough. Pete had showed me how to patch just in time, like someone's looking out for me.

Now I prayed that the repair would hold until we got to port. Even at half speed, we could pull into Rupert this very day. I guess that was the idea of us taking the short cut in the first place.

When Pete brought my meal of biscuits and bacon I knew

I'd not received credit for patching the damaged hull. I'd been put back on cold, rough food. I'd just finished the last swallow with a swig of water when I heard the sound of feet running on the deck . . . preparations for landing. The engines were cut, and we glided up to our berth at the dock.

Prince Rupert, like Bellingham, supplied coal and water to steamers. During the loading, my handkerchief helped to filter out the coal dust that swirled around below decks. But then Pete called me to help shovel coal forward from under the coal chute. Afterwards my porthole was on the wrong side for seeing much of the bustling Canadian port. Two carpenters came on board and fashioned a better patch on the damaged hull. Then we quickly pulled away from the dock and again headed north; this time bound directly for Ketchikan in the United States Territory of Alaska.

thirty-seven

A PAIN IN MY SIDE

Four hours out of Prince Rupert, we put into a small bay and dropped anchor. Pete tended the boiler during the night, so I took the first full shift at sunrise.

As I slid out of my bunk, I doubled over with a sharp pain in my side. I paused to give it time to pass, but it continued to hurt without let-up.

I had to get aft and relieve Pete. Clawing my way in desperation, I crawled up the catwalk over the coal bunker into the boiler room. With intense effort, I straightened up so as not to let on to Pete I had a problem.

"Time to get up steam," Pete said, heading for his bunk. "The captain'll be calling for full speed ahead any minute now . . . you best be ready."

Pleased that Pete hadn't seen my tears of pain, I picked up the shovel. Even empty it increased my misery. How could I stoke the fire like this? With gritted teeth, and every motion a torment, I managed four shovelfulls but then stopped, gasping for air. Tears mingled with sweat as I leaned on the shovel that had become my instrument of torture.

The shriek of a whistle broke into my thoughts. In seconds I picked up the speaking tube and got the call to reverse engines. The piston rods jumped into motion and the Belle began to move away from the dock. Minutes later, the call came for FULL AHEAD and, as I smoothly shifted into running speed, I realized that now it was up to me to keep up a full head of steam.

As I picked up the shovel, I wondered, why the pain? Then the thought struck like lightning. Appendicitis! If the stabbing pain in my side meant appendicitis, I knew that I would need an operation. If the infected appendix wasn't removed, it would burst and I'd die of blood poisoning. And then, if I did have the operation and went back to shoveling coal too soon . . .

My dad, my faithful father . . . now I know how it must have been for him.

So what could I do now? I looked up at the pressure gauge. It read 180. I had to feed the firebox steadily for the next twenty minutes at least.

I began anew. After five more shovelfulls I dropped to the floor convulsed by pain and cramping; my last shovel of coal spilled on the deck. I simply could do no more. Over and over I called for Pete to help. Several minutes later, writhing in agony, I rolled over and looked at the gauge. It read 160! We were losing our head of steam! I screamed for Pete until I was hoarse. Then the engine stopped! !

After a few seconds of silence, I heard a roar of rage and the Snapper's heavy steps thumping across the deck on his way down. When he found me on the floor, he roared again and spewed a steady streak of the worst swearing I'd ever heard . . . directed at me.

Blue eyes blazing and red hair flaming, he yelled, "Get up, ya lazy lout! Ya've lost our steam! We're adrift in the channel with no power."

I cringed as he whipped out his strap. He screeched hysterically, "Get up and stoke that boiler or we'll run aground with the current!"

The tongue-bashing was bad enough, but worse by far, was the leather strap that lashed out time after time, biting into my bare flesh like a branding iron searing my back and shoulders. I thought I'd die right then.

When Pete ran in, the Captain charged back up to the wheel-house as I lay curled up – a helpless heap, moaning in misery.

Then came the welcome sound of the shovel as the master stoker took over. I'd saved us yesterday, now he rescued the Belle from disaster by quickly feeding dozens of heaping shovel-fulls into the firebox. The engines snorted steam as the pressure picked up. Half an hour later, Pete had worked the pressure up to 230 and the Belle cruised safely up mid-channel at FULL AHEAD.

Pete pulled the stool over to sit beside me.

"What's ailin' ya, Casey?" he asked.

"Pete," I said, clutching my left side. "I think I have appendicitis."

"Yer pain's there on your left side?"

"Yes." Again, I thought of my dad. "I don't know if I'm going to make it . . . unless I can find a doctor."

"Hey kid, I'll take over your shovelin' for a day or two. You should be O.K. by then. You've pulled a muscle from jamming that brace against the hull yesterday."

"Pulled muscle?" I blinked away tears. "Not appendicitis?"

"Naw, yer pain's on the left. The appendix is on the right."

That simple fact brought great relief. I sobbed a prayer of thanks and silently thought, "I'm going to make it!"

Pete took a minute away from the boiler to smear salve on the welts Snapper had raised. As I lay on my stomach in my bunk, I thanked God again for Pete's double kindness to me. What a friend!

thirty-eight

MY ESCAPE PLAN

My life aboard the Belle had been getting better. I'd learned the stoker's job, found a porthole to look out on the parade of natural wonders, and had enjoyed good food. Now I'd lost it all. Stuck in the smelly hold, confined to my bunk, on my stomach at that, I lay in pitch darkness. Overcome by deep depression, I despaired of ever getting back to K2 and my family. An effort to think of Lobo didn't raise my spirits this time. The side pain, a little better now, flared up when I moved. But the back pain, thanks to our violent captain, felt like eternal fire, making sleep almost impossible. Now that I wasn't working, my meals were cut to two a day; a biscuit and a greasy slice of bacon in the morning and, hours later, a plate of beans.

I'd lost track of time, but at six bells I roused up from a fitful sleep to hear voices in the engine room. With an effort, I made my way aft and found Pete showing Bruce how to stoke the firebox.

I put my head down and thought, "Having Bruce help out takes the pressure off Pete. But I felt a twinge of fear, too. I'd been replaced. I didn't have a job. How long would the Captain carry me . . . a useless crew member?"

Another worry cropped up. When we got to Ketchikan, Snapper might send a ransom note to Uncle Carl. Maybe he already had. Somehow I had to get away and send word back to Seattle.

How could I do that? Pete might help me actually mail it, but somehow I'd have to write a note. My pay envelope! Mr. Clodel had put my pay in an envelope and I still had it somewhere. With trembling hands I searched my jacket and found it folded up in a front pocket. It had the return address of the cannery in the corner. Now I needed something to write with.

Pete entered and sat on his bunk.

In the lantern's light he smiled. "I got the other new guy stokin' coal fer all he's worth."

"Glad he's helping you, but now that I'm out of a job, what's the captain going to do with me?"

"Well, I don't know. He's not one to carry useless cargo. If you can't work, he may jus' pitch you over the side."

I knew Pete had said that to get a rise out of me, but I didn't appreciate his gallows humor.

"So one day I help save the Belle and the crew from winding up in Davey Jones' locker at the bottom of the sea, and the next day I'm about to be sent there. ."

Pete grinned, "That's life aboard a fishing boat. Ya pulls yer weight or ya makes way for the next guy."

"Pete, when we get to Ketchikan, will you help me mail a note to my folks in Seattle?"

Pete looked serious now. "Maybe. What are ya gonna say in the note?"

"Just that I'm alive and I'll get back to them when I can."

"It'd be risky, but I'll do it. I owe you for stopping the leak in the hull, and you need a break right now."

"Good! If I can find a pencil and a scrap of paper, I'll address this envelope. All you'll have to do is put a stamp on the envelope with my note in it, and drop it in the mail."

Pete reached over, and brought out a pencil and paper from his sea bag. I wrote the note just as I told Pete I would, nothing more, and signed it. I prayed that it would reach Uncle Carl and the news would serve to relieve everybody about me.

With Pete's promise of help, I could take my mind off my misery by making plans for an escape when we reached port.

Pete put my letter in his bag and asked, "What do ya know about Ketchikan?"

"Only that as a little coastal settlement on the southern end of the Alaska panhandle, it got very lively when gold was discovered up here."

"Yeah, but not like farther up at Skagway. That was the jumpin' off place for most of the gold-crazy guys coming up through these same waters we're sailing right now. Gold fever sent the price of passage shootin' up. A stinkin' cattle boat that had room for maybe fifty people, would take on over five hundred passengers."

My interest in Alaska soared. I wondered if I'd get to see much of it, even from my porthole . . . unless I escaped while we were tied up at the wharf in Ketchikan.

Again Pete took the lantern with him. He had his hands full bringing Bruce up to speed as a stoker. In the two days that followed, my side and the welts on my back began to heal, but the food got worse. Pete came twice a day now with a meager plate of cold beans. Even the water in my jug was brackish with the taste of coal dust. Now pangs of hunger were added to my ordeal. Certainly 18th-century British sailors had fared better in Spanish prisons than I did in my dark prison below decks on the Belle.

Benny, noteworthy by his absence, probably basked in the captain's favor. He must be feeling guilty . . . taking credit due to me for the quick action with caulk and brace. In this I saw first-hand how a man can change under the influence of a tyrant.

Aboard ship a captain's authority is near absolute, and had been for centuries. In the tight little world of a fishing boat, a crew member's fortunes would rise or fall at the whim of the man in charge. To lose favor in his sight could tumble a crew member's standing to that of a galley slave. So I held no grudge against Benny.

My poor state at least provided much uninterrupted time to devise a plan of escape. I'd only been on deck once, when I took my cold bath in the bay back at Powell Inlet. Now I searched my memory. What had I seen? When the time came to escape, I needed to get around quickly up there.

I drew a sketch in my mind of what I remembered. As I had come up out of the hatch, I'd been attracted by the view out across the water, but I also noted the rail that ran from bow to stern on both sides. Another hatch lay forward. That, of course, would be the one above the coal bunker. At the stern, the transom stood out in my memory because it gave me the step down for my dip in the bay. But what lay just over the rudder? Something . . . an object of some sort, had lain on the fantail of the boat just below a large fishing-net reel. I bounced impatiently on my bunk, but the image of that object wouldn't focus in.

Then my brain projected an unbidden view of Vernon's sneering face in the darkness. But I made it work for me. Instead of resisting it, which I knew would only make the apparition more intense, I smiled and used it to put the missing object I sought to the back of my mind. Perhaps by indirection I would eventually remember it.

When Vernon's face laughed at me, I just let the image be. When he hid from me in the forest, I walked on to face him.

Yes, he'd hidden from me, and hiding had worked. Now, if I get on deck, I needed to hide. But where?

Then the elusive mystery object I'd sought sprang into focus. A lifeboat! Lying across the stern, an inverted lifeboat completed my mental sketch of the deck. If I crawled underneath, it would be a perfect place to hide until I could make my way to the wharf.

But a diversion of some kind would be needed . . . some action that would distract the crew's attention away from me. A fire in the coal bunker would certainly divert the crew. But no. That would be more of a diversion than I'd need, too hazardous. I didn't want to destroy the Belle, just escape from her.

Hmm, that gave me an idea. I needed to get on deck before hiding in the lifeboat. The hatch above my bunk would be barred at night. Now that we had a full load of coal, why not simply climb up the coal from the boiler room to the underneath side of the hatch, raise it up, and climb out on deck? Of course! A plan was taking shape.

Timing, precise timing of events would be important. I decided to make my move just as we pulled into Ketchikan. Each member of our small crew would be busily involved in the docking routine.

thirty-nine

KETCHIKAN FACE-OFF

Huge flocks of seabirds filled the sky ahead, the first sign that a bustling fishing village lay just up the channel. The hatch lay partly open and their pulsating cry penetrated down to me . . . I was filled with the urge to be free of my dank prison.

"Oh! To be like a bird, flying out there in the fresh, cool sea breeze!" The thought made me shiver in anticipation. I sensed the time to break free would come soon.

Minutes later I could hear the scramble of feet on the deck. Someone slammed the hatch shut above. Ha! They're not taking a chance with me jumping ship. But they don't suspect I've devised another way out.

The Belle being about to be tied up at dock, I was prompted to get moving. Eager to act, I forced myself to stay calm: "I'll lie low for a few more minutes, just to be sure."

The captain shouted, "Make her fast, fore and aft!"

Time to go. I made a shape of myself under the blanket with the second blanket and the clothes I wasn't wearing. In the light of the lantern, it would appear that I still slept there in my bunk. I'd been served my plate of beans some time ago, so it might be hours before they discovered my absence.

I pulled on my sweater and cap, then moved silently to the coal bunker. I still had a dull side ache and the angry welts on my back made it painful for me to crawl up the pile of coal. It was high time I got out of this miserable place!

Bracing my shoulder under the hatch, I pushed, raising it slightly . . . but it became clear that I needed something to pry with. The shovel! Just the thing.

I slid back down to the deserted boiler room, and picked up the shovel and a bucket to use as a prop. I used the shovel to pry the hatch open and the bucket to hold the space for me. I slid out and lay on the deck, hardly wanting to breathe for fear of attracting attention. I heard the crew inside the main cabin celebrating the end of their long journey north, so there wasn't much chance I'd be seen. I rose up, slipped the bucket out, let it slide back on the coal with the shovel, and gently lowered the hatch.

Skidoo! The first part of the plan had gone perfectly. I slithered on my stomach across the deck to the lifeboat. Would there be room under the edge for me to climb under? Yes . . . and, as I put my legs under, I stopped, transfixed by the sight of MY UNCLE CARL WALKING UP THE GANGPLANK with a man in uniform.

It was evening, but the sky still glowed with the sun's last rays, and with eyes unused to light, I squinted at the sight of Captain Dunn swaggering up to confront Carl Coleman.

"Stop! You've no right to board my boat!" he shouted.

The uniformed man replied, "I'm Deputy Blainstock, this man's from Seattle and claims you kidnapped his nephew."

Flabbergasted, I wondered how Uncle Carl had traveled up here so quickly . . . in time to meet us when we docked. He must have come by the fast passenger steamer that had passed by our slower boat.

About to jump up and run to the men who were talking

about me, I paused when I heard the captain's calm reply.

Holding the paper I'd signed in Uncle Carl's face, he said: "Look at this. If Casey Jones is the one you're lookin' fer, he's legally hired on as an able-bodied seaman. Here's his application that he signed in front of me and witnessed by seaman Ben Vanderhorn here. All proper and legal it is."

Uncle Carl glared at the captain. "My nephew isn't 18. This document is worthless."

Captain Dunn raised his bushy eyebrows. "Oh? Well I just took his word for that. I suppose you have proof that he hain't as old as he sez. You have his birth certificate, maybe?"

"No."

The captain sensed victory. "You don't? Well then Casey Jones stays with me."

Uncle Carl sputtered, "But . . . but you forced Casey to sign that paper. Get him out here, let's see what he says."

"Forced? You hear that, Mr. Vanderhorn? Did anyone force our Casey to sign this? Certainly not. He came asking for work and he's turned out to be a good stoker."

The deputy shook his head. "Well, Mr. Coleman, I'm afraid the law is on their side unless you can disprove their claim."

"Right you are!" roared the captain. "Now back off this gang-plank."

Uncle Carl turned with clenched fists and trotted back down to the dock with the deputy following. To make matters worse, the captain taunted them with a long, raucous laugh.

He called out, "Haw, haw . . . I see why Casey run off from the likes of you, Mister Coleman, cannery man. He's better off with me."

That made me cringe. With the welts on my back stinging still, I decided to make a break for it.

But Bruce beat me to it. In a sudden, surprise move, he shot out of the hold, raced to the gangplank, pushed the startled captain out of the way and ran for freedom.

Everyone watched in disbelief as Red Snapper stopped his jeering, teetered on the edge, and, with arms waving in desperation, pitched backward into the icy waters below.

As Benny ran to pick up a line to throw to his captain, I too ran over and down the gangplank.

Uncle Carl and the deputy, now on the dock, jumped in amazement as Bruce sped past. They heard the captain's big splash and turned, astounded, to see yet another young man running toward them. Wild-eyed, and bedraggled, my figure must have seemed bizarre in the extreme. I called out, "Thanks for coming," ran right past them and on to dry land, shouting, "Free! I'm really free!"

… # forty

SAILING SOUTH IN STYLE

As I lounged in a deck chair . . . without a care or concern, I allowed my thoughts to travel back to events after leaving Seattle. In contrast to my outward calm, my brain worked furiously . . . stoking my consciousness with a panorama of vivid images. As in a movie theater, I relaxed, and, in perfect comfort, watched a re-play of "Life Aboard the Silver Belle" roll before my inner eye.

I was back in the engine room. On this cool day, I nevertheless felt the constant heat radiating from the boiler, and the odor of smoke lingered in my nostrils. Tension built up. What was the steam pressure? The gauge! Check the gauge! But then someone's voice broke in.

"Excuse me, sir. May I offer you a bit of refreshment from the galley?"

Here, on the open deck of Sitka Seafarer, with Uncle Carl snoring softly near by, I took note of the waiter patiently standing at my elbow. I'd noticed him, in shiny black shoes and white uniform, serving tea and sandwiches on a silver tray and had thought, "as shipboard duties go, catering to passengers sure beats a stoker's job."

I dreamily responded, "Why, yes. Might I have a coffee

with a touch of sugar?"

"A coffee with sugar? Of course, sir, may I also suggest just a bit of whipped cream topping?"

"Yes. I'd like that . . . and perhaps another of those delicious chocolate eclairs I had at breakfast."

"Yes sir. Would there be anything else?"

"Nothing more."

Before the waiter returned, I surveyed the pristine beauty of numerous forested islands as we passed by and I gave a deep sigh of satisfaction. Light streaming through the tips of the trees, shimmering on the water, distracted me from previous thoughts that had been burned into my mind. The dark days under the domination of Captain Dunn would take time to fade from the forefront of my mind. The pleasantries afforded me as a first-class passenger on this voyage back to Seattle, however, were building a new set of memories.

The refreshments arrived and were placed before me with practiced ease. I nodded and began to sip coffee. As I drank it, my thoughts shifted to the events following my escape.

Uncle Carl had taken me to lodgings in a boarding house. The elderly landlady, Mrs. Doyle, had drawn a bath for me, and for the next hour I had scrubbed, cleaned, and shampooed the grime from my body.

Not knowing what to expect in Ketchikan, I was pleased to discover the indoor plumbing and steaming hot water. Certainly an improvement over what I had heard was available during the Gold Rush days.

Uncle Carl had brought the only doctor in town over to tend to my inflamed back. Lucky for me, only one of the welts had become infected, and it responded to treatment.

While applying soothing lotion to my welts, Uncle Carl had grumbled and muttered plans to "track down" that "Captain Bligh" and "put him on trial." I certainly agreed that Red

Snapper belonged behind bars.

I had used Uncle Carl's shaving cream mug and brush, spreading hot lather all over my face. This wasn't really necessary, because my beard had sprouted only on my chin and upper lip. But I loved the luxurious, hot, foamy feel of it. Then I'd used Uncle Carl's straight razor to shave, nicking my chin only slightly. I'd left my sideburns long, pleased to note the scar on my cheek had receded.

Mrs. Doyle, as handy with a barber's scissors as she was knowledgeable of Gold Rush times, spoke of days past while giving me an Alaskan style, longer than usual, haircut. Afterwards, I suppose, I looked normal again, except that the tan I'd acquired at K2 had faded.

While Uncle Carl and I waited the eight days for the Sitka Seafarer to return from its latest Seattle run, we had time to look for Bruce. It seemed unwise for me to appear in public, even though Silver Belle had hurriedly left port minutes after Bruce and I had escaped. But Uncle Carl inquired around town for Bruce and didn't find him. The way he'd sped down the dock, he might be running yet.

As I mentally closed the chapter of my life aboard the Silver Belle, and said good bye to Pete, I thought of the old adage, "a friend in need is a friend indeed."

I'd decided to use this time not only to tend my scarred back, but to talk at length to the living historian, Mrs. Doyle. In 1897, the landlady and her husband had set up a thriving business in Skagway, selling supplies shipped up from Seattle and Tacoma.

She told amazing stories of the thousands that had landed seeking gold. Some of them were surprised to find that their destination, the Klondike gold fields, weren't in Alaska, but in the Yukon Territory that lay east, over the border into Canada, and then miles to the north. To get there, the would-be miners learned they had to climb a steep mountain over White Pass, up the trail from Skagway, or Chilkoot Pass up beyond Dyea, into British Columbia. From there, both of these trails crossed over into the vast Yukon Territory.

I listened to Mrs. Doyle tell her adventurous true tales for hours at a time. She described how the newcomers had to leave the ships they came on at the edge of a sand flat . . . there being no dock . . . and had to be quick to get their belongings ashore before the tide came in.

The get-rich-quick folks were heading up to Dawson, the town in the Klondike region. They'd heard, rightly, that tons of gold had been mined and panned there. But at both Chilkoot Pass and also at White Pass, the Canadian Mounted Police would not let anyone into Canada unless they brought with them a ton of supplies, enough to last them six months in Dawson. So those who traveled up the trail to the passes, packed about fifty pounds of food and goods on their backs at a time. Upon reaching the top, they would stack their goods, mark it somehow, and go back for another fifty pounds. After forty round trips they'd have collected the ton of supplies. Some had horses or dogs that helped move supplies. Many of these poor animals were worked to death, or slipped off the trail and died from the fall.

As I listened to Mrs. Doyle, it struck me that the most amazing part of this saga of those times, were the trails themselves. Out of either Skagway or nearby Dyea, after the first few miles, the trails shot up at a steep thirty-five degree angle that was difficult for all and impossible for some. Those who found the climb totally exhausting dumped their equipment or, if lucky, sold their supplies for ten cents on the dollar and turned back. Gold-seeking was hazardous. Many died of disease or froze to death in snowstorms. Over a period of three years, a hundred thousand traveled to Alaska seeking their fortunes, and about half of them made it up to Dawson.

Mrs. Doyle ended the story with details of the last five-hundred-mile leg of the journey up to Dawson. This involved the headwaters of the Yukon River and several lakes. To sail them, the travelers cut timber, sawed it into planks, and built boats. When the stalwart gold-seekers finally arrived at their destination, some early ones found gold. Most of them, however, found the town over-run with disappointed would-be miners, looking for a way to get back home.

When once again my thoughts returned to my pleasant Sitka Seafarer journey, my present state was in stark contrast to the ordeal of those who had sought the bonanza of the Yukon. Next to me, Uncle Carl awoke, possibly due to the smell of fresh coffee. He called the waiter to bring a cup for himself as well.

"So, how are you doing, Casey? You feeling back to normal and all?"

I would never be exactly be the same, but I answered, "Yes, this cruise is so very pleasant, it's medicine for both body and soul."

Uncle Carl chuckled at this. "Well, we'll soon have you back in Seattle. Min will be overjoyed to see you looking so well. When we dock, I'll send a telegram to your Uncle Harry."

Just then, a man somewhat younger than Uncle Carl leaned over from the adjoining table.

"Pardon the interruption, I'm Lear Bennett. I'm a geologist from the University of Washington."

We soon introduced ourselves and asked Mr. Bennett to join our little table.

"I've made this trip back and forth to Ketchikan several times this year while writing up my mineral surveyor's reports. I'm pleased to have someone from Seattle to talk with."

With his boots, open-necked shirt and mackinaw, Mr. Bennett looked to be the typical, rugged, outdoors type. He spoke enthusiastically about Alaska's future.

"Yes, in 1867, when our government bought the territory of Alaska from Russia for a mere $7,200,000, many called it a worthless 'ice box.' But let me tell you, I've found it to be as rich in resources as anywhere in the world. Along with the Klondike strike, gold was discovered in Nome, Fairbanks and other places too. Alaska has deposits of copper, nickel, tin, lead, and zinc."

I broke in. "Mr. Bennett, it's great to hear more about this part of the world. While in Ketchikan I heard mostly about the Gold Rush times, and I couldn't see much because it was mostly cloudy."

"Unfortunate for you. Maybe some time on a return trip you'll see more of this great land. I'm amazed at Alaska's sheer scenic beauty . . . the endless forests, glaciers and inlets dazzle the eye."

Mr. Bennett went on enthusiastically. "There's a growing interest in the salmon that swim up the many rivers to spawn. In season, they're so thick you can almost walk on them."

At the mention of salmon, Uncle Carl asked, "Mr. Bennett, I'm in the salmon canning business in Seattle. Should I be concerned about competition from Alaska?"

"My prediction is that in the years to come, over-fishing in Puget Sound will be a greater factor, true for Bellingham as well."

"I lived in New York City in my early years," I began. "I really had no awareness of Alaska and its potential."

"Potential is the perfect one-word description of it. A young man, like yourself, might be interested in building a life in this sparsely populated north country. What opportunities there are! Just think of the sheer size of it . . . over twice the size of Texas, with twelve of the highest peaks in North America."

The next day I met another interesting personality on board. Uncle Carl took me up to the top deck to meet the captain. He turned out to be the opposite of Captain Dunn. A true gentleman, he invited us to the bridge, where we got an even more magnificent view of the inlets and channels of the Inside Passage.

The captain asked: "Like to take the wheel, Casey?"

"Oh, yes sir. Will you tell me what to do?"

"Yes, of course, just hold her steady. You'll notice that though we're on a straight heading, we still need to carry a little rudder."

I felt the need to put a little pressure on the wheel to keep the Sitka Seafarer on course. "Why is that?" I asked.

"Because we must compensate for a light current that would otherwise pull us slightly to starboard."

"I see," I said knowingly.

At that moment, the captain turned aside to Uncle Carl for a moment. "Your nephew may have the makings of a seafaring man."

Just then, a black and white whale leaped from the water just in front of us and I instinctively turned the wheel in order to miss it. The captain sprang back and took charge, slowly turning the wheel back to resume our true course.

After a minute, he chuckled, "Well, that was a surprise. You reacted quickly there, Casey."

Embarrassed and wondering if I had done the right thing, I asked, "Do you think that whale would have gotten out of our way if I hadn't turned the ship?"

The captain smiled, "Yes, that was one of those playful orcas we frequently see up here. I think he wanted to get a reaction from us. But there's no harm in trying to avoid a collision, is there?"

At that remark, I again thought of my namesake, the railroad engineer. This had to be the last place I'd expected to be reminded of him.

forty-one

A CHANGE OF HEART

The months that followed my return to Seattle were relatively uneventful. Mom decided to postpone her move to Arborville, and I decided to celebrate Christmas with Uncle Carl and Aunt Min. On my first day back, Gene, Veronica and Janet had hit me with a constant barrage of questions. I enjoyed being the center of attention, and it pleased me no end to hear that only three days before my return, Sniggy had left Webster High because his family had moved to California.

I looked forward to June, and my return to Arborville. When the day arrived, Uncle Carl and Aunt Min, Gene, Veronica and Janet all came to the King Street Station to see me off. They made me promise to come back for visits.

I boarded the train, this time to travel back to the place that I now thought of as home: the sprawling, friendly and somewhat wild K2 ranch.

At dawn the next morning Jasper and I cantered out toward the brilliant rays of the rising sun. The air, even more fragrant than I'd remembered it, streamed through my hair, and I shivered with delight as a covey of quail loudly fluttered out beside the trail.

Yesterday as I'd jumped off the train, Uncle Harry had

grabbed me in a big bear hug and Aunt Louise and the girls had showered me with hugs and kisses. What a greeting! But then the Kinsman family released me into the arms of my mom.

A bit grayer now, smiling and looking so beautiful, she too held me tight.

"Oh my Casey!" she said. "How could you have grown up so quickly? You got on the train a boy and now just look at you! You've become a young man."

I loved the memory of the day before, but now, as Jasper veered up into the woods toward Cal's hideaway, I enjoyed our swift motion up the trail and breathed deeply the scented forest air.

I touched the scar on my face. Yes, I'd changed since I'd left Mom in New York and headed west. I flexed my arms, hardened from hurling tons of coal into the breech aboard the Belle, and I eagerly anticipated learning more about ranching and working here, protecting the Kinsmans' interests in every way I could.

I re-lived the events of last night, especially the joyful dinner at Overton Manor, everyone celebrating my home-coming. We'd had prime rib roast, with corn on the cob and fresh peas from Annie's garden, topped off with Aunt Louise's deep-dish apple pie and home-made ice cream with fresh strawberries. What a feast!

I tried not to talk about my experiences aboard the Belle. So when Colette had asked, "Casey, did you catch a lot of halibut while you were aboard the fishing boat?" I answered, "No, I just caught a lot of hell from the captain!"

Despite the evident stark truth of it, everyone roared with laughter, and there were no more allusions to my fishing boat life . . . that is, until the next day when I went swimming with the cousins.

I should have prepared them for the awful sight of my

back, healed now but still scarred. Neva and Colette paled with shock, simply struck speechless, while Annie put her head on my shoulder, and cried as she gently hugged me. "Oh, Casey," she sobbed. "We hadn't any idea it had been so bad . . . so brutal for you on board." She stepped back, wiped a tear and looked me in the eye. "Now I know our prayers helped bring you back to us."

After dinner we'd all had a songfest. Aunt Louise and Neva traded off on the piano and I belted out one tune after another on the guitar, finishing the happy session with three verses of "Wabash Cannonball."

Near bedtime, Mom and I got a chance to chat. She mentioned selling off her last few pieces of furniture, and packing up her possessions. Before leaving for Grand Central Station, she had stopped once more at the cemetery to remember Dad, then had taken the train as I had done.

Just before I left for my room, I brought up the question that'd been on my mind for several months.

"Mom," I began. "Aunt Min mentioned that one of the Kinsman girls is adopted, but she wouldn't say which one."

Mom laughed. "Yes, it's true, and I'm laughing because I imagine you're quite curious to know."

"Mom!" I said, blushing in spite of myself. "Come on! Don't tease me about this. I'd simply like to know which one is adopted, Neva, Colette, or Annie."

"I've noticed you looking at them. Can't you see the family resemblance?"

"No! I mean yes!" My head felt like Belle's boiler about to blow.

Then Mom finally came out with it.

"You can't tell by looking, because none of them is adopted. But Minnie told the truth. You see, Casey, I'm the adopted Kinsman girl."

• • •

Jasper whinnied and slowed to a trot as we neared the hideaway. As the reality of what Mom had revealed last night sank in, I felt relieved. Now, my feelings for my step-cousins could take on a more natural aspect. We were all quite young to be thinking seriously about the friendship I had with each of them. But who knows what the future might bring?

Never before had my heart been so filled with gratitude. As one of two young men who'd jousted in a struggle to the death, I'd met, to quote the Bard, 'the slings and arrows of outrageous fortune,' and with the help of a friend and the love of a dog I'd survived.

Humbly I lifted my spirit in a fervent prayer of thanks and ended with, "Lord, please stay with me for the challenges that lie ahead."

I pulled up, leaned back and sent a shortened cry of the goshawk into the air.

I heard it returned and thrilled to the promise that lay before me.

"They're waiting to welcome us back to the hideaway, Jasper. Soon I'll run with Lobo, and later, as the shadows dance before us, I'll drink coffee from a tin cup and tell tales of Alaska. And, by firelight, Cal will spin the ancient stories I so love to hear, of goshawks, wolves and other creatures in the wild."

I knew this because just then, a real birdcall pierced the morning mist. Jasper shivered and my heart rose within me as the true, drawn out, cry of the goshawk was heard throughout the forest and echoed in the hills beyond.

THE HIDEAWAY